Victoria felt another hot flush fill her cheeks. How dared he order her about as if she were his middy? Jacob Carstairs, with his impertinent ways and too-bright gray eyes that seemed to see everything, needed a lesson in manners. He ought to learn that young men who wore their collar points too low and who teased young ladies to whom they were not even related would never earn the affection of anyone . . . particularly any of those said young ladies.

And Victoria thought she knew just who could best give this lesson to the unfortunate captain.

Accordingly, she turned to Lord Malfrey, and, giving him her hand once more, said gravely, "My lord, in answer to your question, I would be *honored* to be your wife."

The look of astonishment that flickered across Captain Carstairs's face at that moment quite made up for Victoria's no longer being able to look forward to Lord Malfrey's leaping overboard in frustrated passion.

In all, she congratulated herself on a job well done. *Very* well done indeed!

DON'T MISS A SINGLE
AVON TRUE ROMANCE

AN AVON TRUE ROMANCE

Victoria
and the
Rogue

MEG CABOT

AVON BOOKS

An Imprint of HarperCollinsPublishers

FIND TRUE LOVE!
www.avontrueromance.com

For Benjamin

ACKNOWLEDGMENTS

Many thanks to Beth Ader, Jennifer Brown, Michele Jaffe, Laura Langlie, and Abby McAden.

CHAPTER ONE

The Atlantic Ocean, Gibraltar, 1810

"Lady Victoria?"

Victoria turned her head at the sound of her name being called so softly from across the ship deck. The moon was full. She could see the person calling to her quite clearly by its silver light . . . but she doubted that he, in turn, would be able to perceive the blush that suffused her cheeks at the sight of him.

Yet how could she help but blush? The sight of the tall, flaxen-haired lord nearly always brought color to her cheeks—not to mention a curious flutter to her pulse. He was so handsome. What woman would *not* blush when such a good-looking man happened to glance her way?

And tonight Lord Malfrey was doing a good deal more than glancing. Indeed, he was crossing the deck to come and stand beside her at the ship railing, where she'd leaned for the past half hour staring at the hypnotic band of light that the moon was casting upon the water, and listening to the gentle lap of waves upon the sides of the *Harmony*, the ship that had carried them all from India.

"Good evening, my lord," Victoria murmured demurely, when the earl reached her side.

"You are well, Lady Victoria?" Lord Malfrey asked with just a hint of anxiety in his deep voice. "Forgive me for asking, but you hardly touched your dinner. And then you left the table before dessert was served."

Victoria did not think it would be at all romantic, standing as they were beneath that lush silver moon, to inform the earl that she'd left the table because the roast had been so scandalously underdone that she'd felt it her duty to go to the galley and have words about it with the cook.

It was not her place, of course, to have done so. Mrs. White, the captain's wife, was the one who ought properly to have taken the ship's cook to task.

But Mrs. White, in Victoria's opinion, would not know a roux from a bearnaise, and quite probably *liked* her meat undercooked. Victoria had never been able to abide slovenly cooking. And it was so simple to do a roast properly!

But this was hardly the kind of thing one brought up before a young man like Lord Malfrey. Not under a night sky like the one above them. Besides, one simply did not speak of underdone meat in front of an earl.

And so instead Victoria said, stretching a hand eloquently toward the moon, "Why, I only wanted a breath of fresh air and happened upon this view. It was so lovely, how could I return below and miss such a breathtaking sight?"

This was, Victoria thought to herself, a bit of a high-flown speech. There were those on board, she knew, who might well make retching noises had they happened to have overheard it.

Fortunately, Hugo Rothschild, the ninth Earl of Malfrey, was not one of those people. His blue-eyed gaze followed the graceful arc of her arm, and he said reverently, "Indeed. I have never seen such a beautiful moon. But"— and here his gaze returned to Victoria—"it is not the only breathtaking sight to be seen here on deck."

Victoria knew she was blushing quite hard now—but from pleasure, not embarrassment. Why, the earl was flirting with her! How perfectly delightful. Her ayah back in Jaipur had warned her that men might try to flirt with her, but Victoria had hardly expected someone as handsome as Lord Malfrey to pay her such civilities. It was beginning to seem as if the evening, which had looked rather dismal in light of the disastrous roast, was shaping up very nicely indeed.

"Why, Lord Malfrey," Victoria said, lowering her sooty eyelashes—though they were not *really* sooty, of course, as Victoria was a scrupulous bather. But they were, or so her ayah had informed her, as black as soot, anyway. "I can't think what you mean."

"Can't you?" Lord Malfrey reached out and suddenly

took the hand that she'd purposefully left lying upon the ship's railing, temptingly close to his. "Victoria—may I call you Victoria?"

He could have called her Bertha and Victoria would not have minded in the least. Not when he was pressing her hand so tightly, as if it were the most precious thing in the world, against his chest. She could feel his heart drumming, strong and vibrant, beneath the cream-colored satin of his waistcoat. *Goodness*, she thought with some astonishment. *I believe he is about to propose!*

Which he promptly did.

"Victoria," Lord Malfrey said, the moonlight bringing into high relief the planes of his regularly featured face. He was such a handsome man, with his square jaw and broad shoulders. He would, Victoria decided with some satisfaction, make a very dashing husband indeed. "I know we have not been acquainted long—just under three months—but these past few weeks . . . well, they've been the happiest I've ever known. It breaks my heart that tomorrow I shall have to leave you to travel on to England alone, for I have business to attend to in Lisbon. . . ."

Dreadful Lisbon! How Victoria hated the sound of that foul city, stealing away this excessively charming young man! Lucky Lisbon, that it should get to bask in the glow of the delightful Lord Malfrey.

"Oh, well," she said, trying to sound airily unconcerned. "Perhaps we shall meet again in London by and by—"

"Not by and by," Lord Malfrey said, flattening her palm against his heart with both hands. "Never say by and by when it concerns us! For I never met a girl quite like you, Victoria, so beautiful . . . so intelligent . . . so competent with the help. I cannot imagine what a perfect creature like you could ever see in a pitiful wastrel like myself, but I promise that if, whilst I am in Lisbon, you will wait for me, and then upon my return deign to give me your hand in marriage, I will love you until the day I die, and do nothing but try to make myself worthy of you!"

La, Victoria thought, very pleased at this turn of events. *How jolly this is! A girl goes to chastise a cook for underdoing the roast, and comes back to the table a bride-to-be!* Her uncle John would be quite put out when he heard about it, however. He'd wagered Victoria wouldn't get a proposal until she'd been at least a year in England, and here she was getting one before even setting foot on shore. He wouldn't be at all happy about owing her uncles Henry and Jasper a fiver.

The three of them would be taught a sharp lesson indeed! Imagine them sending her off to England so unceremoniously, simply because she had suggested—merely suggested, mind you—that one of them marry her dear friend Miss . . . Oh, what was her name again, anyway? Well, it was simply ridiculous, not one of them agreeing to marry poor Miss Whatever-Her-Name-Was, when Victoria had had such a lovely wedding planned. Now it was her own wedding she'd be planning instead! Perhaps when her uncles caught a glimpse of her own wedded bliss, they'd give Miss Whatever-Her-Name-Was a second look. . . .

"Oh, dear," Victoria said in tones of great—and completely feigned—distress, batting those sooty lashes as her ayah had recommended. "This is all so terribly sudden, Lord Malfrey."

"Please," Lord Malfrey said, clutching her hand even more tightly, if such a thing were possible. "Call me Hugo."

"Very well . . . Hugo," Victoria said in her most womanly voice. "I . . ."

It was always a good idea, Victoria's ayah had told her, to leave young men in some suspense as to your true feelings for them. Accordingly, Victoria was about to tell young Lord Malfrey that his ardor had taken her completely unawares, and that as she was but sixteen and hardly yet ready for matrimony, she'd have to turn down his kind proposal . . . for now. With any luck, this answer would throw the poor young man into such a fit of passion that he might do something rash, such as heave himself overboard, which would be very exciting indeed. And if he survived the dunking, Victoria would be assured of a good many more proposals from him when he returned from Portugal, which would give her something to look forward to whilst she was staying with her horrid aunt and uncle Gardiner.

All of her hopes for a dramatic—and hopefully very

damp—climax to this tender scene were dashed, however, when, just as Victoria was about to turn down Lord Malfrey's proposal, a deep and all-too-familiar voice reached her from across the ship's deck, its accents, as always, dripping with sarcasm.

"There you two are," Jacob Carstairs drawled as he stepped out of the shadows by the rigging and into the silver puddle of light thrown by the moon. "The captain was wondering— Oh, I say, I'm not *interrupting* anything, am I?"

Victoria snatched her hand out from beneath the earl's grip. "Certainly not," she said quickly.

Stuff and bother! What a tiresome young man this Jacob Carstairs was! Since he'd joined the *Harmony* at the Cape of Good Hope six weeks earlier, he seemed always to be appearing at the most inopportune times, such as whenever Victoria and the earl happened to find a rare moment alone together.

And it wasn't as if Captain Carstairs—for in spite of his youth, the interfering young gentleman was a naval officer—were so very pleasing a companion. Why, he wore his collar points shockingly low, instead of level with the corners of his mouth, as Lord Malfrey and all the most stylish young men were wearing them. And he had been exceedingly disrespectful to Victoria the time he had overheard her advising Captain White that his crew would be a good deal less discontented if they were only made aware of the merits of higher thought. Victoria herself had volunteered to read to them every noontide from Mary Wollstonecraft's *Vindication of the Rights of Women*, and had been a good deal put out when Captain White politely declined her kind offer.

Mr. Carstairs, however, had not been a bit polite about it. He had taken to calling her Miss Bee—as in busy bee— and had ventured that if she was always this intent on offering her assistance to people who hadn't asked for it, it was no wonder her bachelor uncles were sending her to live with relatives back in England.

And yet here Jacob Carstairs was, butting his nose into the private affairs of his fellow ship passengers! Why, it was infuriating!

Lord Malfrey seemed to think so, too, if his next words were any indication.

"Actually, Carstairs," the earl said in his smooth, cultured tone, "you *are* interrupting something."

"So sorry," Jacob Carstairs said, not sounding the tiniest bit sorry. "But Mrs. White wants Lady Victoria."

"Kindly tell Mrs. White I shall be there directly," Victoria said, straightening her lace fichu, and hoping that perhaps in the moonlight Mr. Carstairs hadn't noticed how very close she and the earl had been standing. . . .

That hope was dashed, however, when Jacob Carstairs said in a tone that sounded not unlike one of her uncles, "No, my lady. You had better go see Mrs. White *now*."

Victoria felt another hot flush fill her cheeks. How

dared he order her about as if she were his middy? Jacob Carstairs, with his impertinent ways and too-bright gray eyes that seemed to see everything, needed a lesson in manners. He ought to learn that young men who wore their collar points too low and who teased young ladies to whom they were not even related would never earn the affection of anyone . . . particularly any of those said young ladies.

And Victoria thought she knew just who could best give this lesson to the unfortunate captain.

Accordingly, she turned to Lord Malfrey, and, giving him her hand once more, said gravely, "My lord, in answer to your question, I would be *honored* to be your wife."

The look of astonishment that flickered across Captain Carstairs's face at that moment quite made up for Victoria's no longer being able to look forward to Lord Malfrey's leaping overboard in frustrated passion.

In all, she congratulated herself on a job well done.

Very well done indeed!

CHAPTER TWO

England!

Victoria gazed at the crowded and busy wharf through the captain's spyglass. So this, she thought, was England at last. She had to confess herself unimpressed. England so far was nothing like her uncles had led her to believe. The dock was almost exactly like the one she'd left in Bombay some three months earlier, being both dirty and exceedingly disorganized-looking. Really, it might almost have *been* Bombay, except for the general dearth of monkeys.

And, of course, there was the fact that above their heads hung a leaden and sullen sky, whilst the sky that had stretched across Victoria's beloved Jaipur had nearly always been cloudless, and as deeply blue as a maharaja's sapphire—except during monsoon season, of course.

Really, it was a lot to ask any girl to bear, this dirty sky and even dirtier dock . . . but it was far, far worse for Victoria, who also had to endure the absence of her fiancé—her secret fiancé—since with the exception of the loathesome Captain Carstairs, no one yet knew Victoria and Lord Malfrey's happy news. Two days! Two whole days since she'd bid the earl farewell! And now they expected her to endure this bleak sky and shoreline as well? No. It was too much.

"Is it the rainy season, then, Captain?" Victoria asked, passing the spyglass back to Captain White, who, along with his wife, had acted as her chaperones throughout the long ocean voyage.

"The rainy season," the captain echoed with a chuckle. "My lady, in England, I am sorry to say, it is never anything but."

Mrs. White, standing beside her husband, looked shocked.

"Percival!" she cried. "Do not quiz Lady Victoria so. Don't you believe a word he says, my lady. It is spring, and while it does rain more than usual in England in the spring, I can assure you that we have our share of fine weather, as well."

Victoria nodded, but could not help darting a dubious look at the sky. If there was a sun behind that thick layer of clouds, she could see no sign of it.

Not that it mattered especially, she thought with an inward shrug. She did not need the sun, after all. She had her own special secret to keep her warm. Though should the sun choose to make an appearance at some point, Victoria would not take it at all amiss.

"Oh, there is the longboat," Mrs. White said, as the sound of a scrape was heard portside. "In a moment the swing will arrive to take you down, my lady. Now, you mustn't be frightened of the swing. It is perfectly safe. You could not be in better hands than the crew of the *Harmony*, as I am certain by now you are well aware. . . ."

But Victoria was hardly paying attention. That was because she had seen, out of the corner of her eye, a bright spot of blue amidst all the monotonous grays and browns that made up the garb of the crew. Only one person on board—with the exception of herself, of course—wore such bold colors, and that was someone Victoria hadn't the slightest interest in speaking to just at that moment—or any moment, to be honest. She turned her face resolutely toward the shoreline, though the damp wind that was tugging on the hem of her pelisse blew from that direction, throwing occasional stinging drops of wet upon her cheeks.

". . . safe as a kitten in a basket," Mrs. White was going on. Then she broke off with a glad cry. "Why, Captain Carstairs! There you are! I was just saying to Lady Victoria that she needn't fear the swing, that in fact it is quite safe. Do reassure her as well, won't you?"

Mr. Carstairs, Victoria noted after the briefest of glances in his direction, still wore the insolent grin he seemed to have had on ever since Lisbon. *Insufferable man!* She pressed her lips together and wished heartily, as she'd been doing ever since that unfortunate incident off the Portuguese coast—where the captain had interrupted her moonlit proposal—that Jacob Carstairs might suffer a shipboard accident that would render him comatose.

Sadly, it did not appear that any such calamity had befallen the young gentleman, since he seemed to have total mastery over his own tongue.

"I am certain," he said in the cool, mocking tone that so infuriated Victoria every time she heard it, "that her ladyship needs no such assurances from me. Any young woman who has been brought up, as Lady Victoria informs me that she has, by four decorated British officers in the wilds of Jaipur—an area, I believe she said, that is rife with tigers—is unlikely to be daunted by a mere swing."

Victoria sent the young man what she hoped he'd read as a scornful look. It was impossible to say what Captain Carstairs would make of her expression, however, since he persisted in seeking her acquaintance despite everything she'd done to discourage him.

"Tigers?" Mrs. White looked horrified. "Really, my lady? I must say, I . . . Tigers? Fearsome creatures, I understand. Are you saying you encountered them? Regularly? How ever did you manage to get away?"

"I shot them, of course," Victoria replied with some asperity, and, at Mrs. White's gasp, flicked an irritated glance in Jacob Carstairs's direction. Honestly, if he wasn't poking fun at Victoria's suggestion to Captain White that the decks be swabbed with lye instead of vinegar so that they'd get cleaner, he was making light of her assertion that lemon juice made the best rinse for ladies' hair.

Apparently lemons were not as bountiful in England as they were in India. But how was she to have known that? He seemed to have an opinion on everything, and not the least compunction about sharing those opinions . . . most especially those for which he had not been asked.

As if this were not irritating enough, Mr. Carstairs had the added fault of looking exceedingly agreeable, despite his distressingly low collar points. His coats and breeches were impeccably tailored, his Hessians highly shined, and his dark hair neatly trimmed. It was quite objectionable that so maddening an individual should be so attractive.

How very different Jacob Carstairs was from a certain other young man Victoria could—but wouldn't, for propriety's sake—name! As different as day and night, though the other gentleman was every bit as handsome . . . but certainly better skilled at turning his shirt collar, as well as holding his tongue.

It was unfortunate that Victoria had not quite mastered that particular art as well, since Mrs. White was all in a dither over her tiger remark.

"Shot them!" Mrs. White cried, her face going white as the lace inside her bonnet. "My lady! With a rifle?"

It occurred to Victoria a bit belatedly that proper young English women did not as a general rule make a habit of going about and shooting wild animals, and that she really ought to have kept this particular talent of hers secret—rather like she was trying to keep secret that particular moonlit night off the coast of Lisbon . . . no thanks to Captain Carstairs, who was forever reminding her of it, as he did so now.

"Oh, Lady Victoria is as skilled at firing a rifle as she is at winning hearts. She has as many tiger pelts as she does marriage proposals," he said with a wink—an actual wink!—in Victoria's direction. "She collects them. Don't you, my lady?"

Victoria was convinced that if there were a ruder young man in all the world, she had yet to encounter him. It was on the tip of her tongue to point this fact out to the impertinent Captain Carstairs when Mrs. White's husband, who'd gone portside to supervise the lowering of the longboat, suddenly reappeared with the announcement, "Lady Victoria, if you are quite ready, the swing has been prepared."

Victoria, still smarting over Jacob Carstairs's reminder of the tender scene he'd so rudely interrupted the other night, replied, without stopping to think what she was saying, "I shan't need the swing, Captain. I am perfectly able-bodied, and shall climb the ladder down to the longboat like everyone else."

Young Captain Carstairs raised his dark eyebrows upon hearing this, but for once said nothing. It was Mrs. White who looked likely to suffer an apoplexy over Victoria's announcement.

"The ladder?" she cried. "The ladder? Oh, my lady,

you can't know . . . you must not be aware . . . the ladder will never do at all. Oh, no, not at all. I cannot allow it. I simply cannot."

Stuff and bother. Belatedly, Victoria realized she had, once again, committed a faux pas. Young English ladies did not apparently climb down ladders, any more than they went strolling around the decks of sailing ships after dark with young men to whom they were not related—as she had had pointed out to her several times, and to her everlasting chagrin, by Jacob Carstairs. It might, Victoria reflected, have been nice if her uncles had warned her of these things before they'd so unceremoniously shipped her off to this bizarre and foreign land.

A glance at Jacob Carstairs, however, showed Victoria that she could not back down now. His gray eyes looked more mischievous than ever, and his mouth was distinctly curled up at the corners.

"Tut, tut, Mrs. White," he said. "Lady Victoria, take the swing? Swings are for mealymouthed misses who swoon at the sight of a shark fin. Lady Victoria is made of much sterner stuff than that. Why, I'd pit her against a shark any day of the week."

Victoria narrowed her eyes at the odious Captain Carstairs. Really, but he was extraordinarily full of himself! Back in Jaipur, if any of the young officers had addressed her in such a manner, Victoria's uncles would have had the unfortunate young man stripped of his rank.

To show Mr. Carstairs that his teasing did not bother her in the least, Victoria turned to Mrs. White and said calmly, "I shan't bang about on a swing in this wind. I'd be dashed along the side of the ship. The ladder will do for me nicely, thank you."

Mrs. White fluttered her hands. "Oh, but my lady, really, I feel I must . . . as your own dear parents are no longer with us, and your uncles appointed me as your guardian for your journey, I feel I must act in their stead, and say that it is truly not at all seemly——"

"Stuff and bother," Victoria said sharply. How tiresome these English ladies were! "Show me the ladder and let us have done with it before the rains come." For the sky overhead definitely looked threatening to Victoria, no matter what anyone else might say, and she did not want her new bonnet, which she'd saved for this very day, to be ruined.

Upon being led to the ladder, however, Victoria found that her enthusiasm for it waned somewhat. It really was quite a long way down, and the ladder was, after all, made only of rope and wood. But, she told herself staunchly, so was the swing, and at least on the ladder she would be in command of her own destiny, whereas the swing would be dropped down by crew members . . . some of whom Victoria feared were not altogether as committed to their duties as one might hope.

Accordingly, she hiked up her skirt and pelisse——

causing Mrs. White to gasp, as if the glimpse of a woman's ankles were quite the most offensive thing in the world. It was a good thing, Victoria thought, that Mrs. White had never been to Jaipur, where women and girls—including Victoria—regularly went about with their feet and legs bared to the knees, and she swung a leg over the ship railing. She teetered there for a moment while her foot sought purchase on the first rung of the rope ladder, and happened to glance down again. . . .

And realized this was a mistake. The men in the boat below looked very small indeed. It was a long, long way down to the water's choppy, whitecapped surface. Such a long way down, in fact, that Victoria began to feel strangely hot, though the wind that was nipping at her skirts was quite brisk. Her pulse, she was convinced, had begun to stagger, and her mouth had gone suddenly very dry.

Victoria froze where she was, beginning to think that the swing might not be such a very bad thing, as at least she could keep her eyes closed all the way down. She was trying to decide how she might broach this subject to the people in front of whom she had only too recently scoffed at such an idea, when she felt a hand, warm and reassuring, upon her gloved fingers.

She opened her eyes to see the odious Captain Carstairs hanging above her, the corners of his lips, as usual, twisted into a smile . . . only this one was not scornful, but rather kind.

"Don't look down," he advised her gently, "and you'll be all right."

Victoria swallowed—a difficulty given the dryness of her throat—and nodded, not trusting her voice. There was nothing for it now. She had no choice but to climb down, as she had apparently lost all ability to speak, and could not ask for the swing.

Down she accordingly went, carefully keeping her gaze on the side of the ship as she climbed. She could hear the men below shouting encouragingly to her—"Easy does it, m'lady," and "Nice 'n' slow now"—and she was quite grateful to them, since their voices made the roaring in her ears, which had nothing to do with the sea, seem less oppressive.

And then finally, sooner than she might have suspected, she felt their hands on her elbows and waist, and she was lifted from the ladder and put down inside the longboat . . . which was a good thing, since her knees gave out completely the moment her feet touched the boat's bottom, and she knew she would not have been able to walk to her seat unaided.

There were some cries of "Hurrah!" from the ship's deck, impossibly high above her head, and Victoria began to feel the blood move inside her veins once more. *La,* she thought. *Why, that was nothing at all! Imagine having been afraid of a little climb like that!*

By the time poor Mrs. White—who, of course, opted to descend by the swing—joined her in the longboat,

Victoria had forgotten all about her own fear and could not help feeling annoyed at the other woman's theatrics. For, despite Mrs. White's assertions that the swing was perfectly safe, she shrieked quite hysterically all the way down, before collapsing completely once she was safely inside the longboat. Victoria was forced to wave hartshorn beneath the lady's nose before she became sensible—quite a deplorable way to behave, Victoria could not help thinking, for a ship captain's wife. She could not see why Captain White bothered to let his wife come along during his voyages at all.

Captain Carstairs, who descended by ladder a few moments after Mrs. White was safely delivered, had nothing but admiring looks for Victoria—something she noted with a good deal of relish. It was a shame about Jacob Carstairs's collar points—and his character, of course, which was of far too teasing a bent to be desirable—because in every other respect he was quite an agreeable young man. In fact, if she hadn't met Lord Malfrey first, Victoria thought she might have found herself in some danger of falling for the dashing captain. . . .

Except, of course, for his grating personal manner, which made any such match unthinkable.

Still, he could be nice enough when he put his mind to it, as he'd illustrated in his sensible advice to Victoria earlier on the deck about not looking down.

At least, that was what Victoria was thinking until the

young captain noticed the hartshorn she held to Mrs. White's pale face. For some reason it compelled Captain Carstairs to remark in a cheerful tone, "Well, you must be feeling very happy indeed, Miss Bee. Finally a chance to be useful to someone!"

From that moment until they safely reached the dock, Victoria had nothing but dark looks for Jacob Carstairs, who enraged her further by seeming only to find her snubs amusing, instead of being upset enough by them to apologize for his rudeness, as any other young man would have done. He showed not the slightest inclination to throw himself overboard in penance for his mistake, either.

As if this were not bad enough, Victoria, upon arriving at last upon the very dirty and disrespectable-looking dock she'd observed through the captain's spyglass, found herself being exhorted by Mrs. White not to stare at the prisoners being loaded onto a ship headed for the penal colonies, something Victoria found very hard not to do, for when else was she ever going to get another chance to look into the face of a tax evader?

But it was not seemly for young English ladies, Mrs. White informed her, to show such avid interest in convicted felons. Back in India, Mrs. White understood, things like public hangings were commonplace, but in England such barbarous activities were no longer tolerated, and hangings took place in prison yards where they belonged, and it was considered rude to stare, even at tax evaders headed for the opposite hemisphere.

What dull creatures the English were! Victoria could
not help thinking. Really, but she found it very difficult
indeed to believe she would ever fit in with these colorless,
bland people. But she supposed that if she was to be married to one of them—though no one could ever think of
Hugo Rothschild as bland—she had better start trying, at
least, to get along with them.

But Victoria felt her patience was being too severely
tested when the loud clattering of horse hooves sounded
on the cobblestones nearby, and she heard her name being
called . . . only, to Victoria's mortification, it was not her
given name being called out, but her nickname.

"Vicky! Vicky!"

Victoria, glancing out from beneath her bonnet brim,
saw a large barouche draw as close to the pier as the street
would allow. Then, before the driver could descend to
open the door, it burst open, and what appeared to be a
veritable flood of children, small animals, and a bare min-
imum of adults came spilling out. All of them began
scrambling toward her, a formidable wall of humanity,
screaming her name.

Victoria, had she been made of less sturdy stuff, might
have turned tail and run from this familial tidal wave. But
she managed to remain calm, and only stepped a little away
from Mrs. White, in order to keep that good lady from
being knocked over in the sea of arms and legs and

upturned faces that soon engulfed Victoria.

"Vicky!" One of the adults, whom Victoria immediately recognized as her mother's sister, her aunt Beatrice Gardiner, flung her arms around her and pulled her into a rib-breaking embrace. "Look at you! Just look at you, all grown up, and looking so very elegant!"

Elegant Victoria supposed she might have looked before that embrace, but she felt her new bonnet slip back from her head just as she was thrust away and held at arm's length by her shoulders while her aunt swiftly assessed her.

"You're every inch of you your father," Mrs. Gardiner exclaimed, her blue-eyed gaze sweeping her niece up and down. "I don't see a single hint of Charlotte in her, do you, Mr. Gardiner?"

Victoria's uncle Walter Gardiner, who had not thrown himself wildly at her like the rest of his family, had instead stood to one side, sucking on his pipe. Now he said only, "Hmmm," and that seemed to be enough to satisfy his wife, who had moved her hands from Victoria's shoulders and was now, to Victoria's abject mortification, running them along Victoria's arms, through the material of her pelisse.

"Look how thin," Mrs. Gardiner exclaimed, with what appeared to be a good deal of satisfaction. "Did your uncles not feed you properly? Oh, I knew it was wrong to leave you there with them. I knew it! And you're so dark! Why, you're tanned dark as a Gypsy! Did your uncles fail to provide you with proper sunshades? And she's so small! Look how small she is, Mr. Gardiner! La, I'd swear she's smaller than Becky, and Becky was the smallest girl at her school. I could put you in my pocket, my dear, and carry you home! And she's still got her father's eyes, I see. Neither brown nor green, but a little of both, as if the good Lord couldn't make up his mind on the matter. And your hair, Vicky, which was so blond when we saw you last. It's turned completely brown! There's not the slightest chance of you and Becky passing for sisters anymore. You're nowhere near alike. Not alike at all!"

While Mrs. Gardiner had been announcing all of this, Victoria was suffering silent throes of agonized embarrassment. It was bad enough to be exclaimed over in such a manner in the privacy of one's own home, but it was ten times more humiliating for it to occur in public . . . and particularly in the presence of one Jacob Carstairs. For Captain Carstairs, Victoria knew—though she dared not glance his way—was somewhere about, and was undoubtedly watching the scene with his customary smirk. To hear her aunt's voice shrieking out her physical flaws like that—and Victoria was very aware that she did have flaws, though she did not consider them quite so serious as her aunt evidently did; she was well aware of her lack of stature, and while she did not think of herself as too thin, she knew she was wanting in certain areas where it was in vogue for young ladies to be well padded—was quite mortifying enough.

But to know that Jacob Carstairs could hear her . . . Well, if Victoria could have chosen to expire on the spot, she would have.

Her cheeks, she knew, were glowing beneath her tan, and she no longer had the brim of her bonnet nor her parasol to hide them beneath: her bonnet was hanging by its ribbons around her neck, and her parasol had been knocked from her hand by her aunt's enthusiastic embrace. She could not, even if she'd wanted to, have raised her gaze to meet Captain Carstairs's, because she would not have been able to see him, so much were her enthusiastic relations crowding her. Her gown and pelisse were being tugged at by a dozen eager hands, as her young cousins vied with one another for her attention. Only one of those cousins did she recognize . . . indeed, the vast majority of them had not yet been born when last Victoria had seen their parents, and that was her cousin Rebecca, who was closest to her own age. It was Rebecca with whom a four-year-old Victoria, along with their parents, had traveled to India, in order that their mothers, who were sisters, might visit their four brothers, stationed in Jaipur with the British military.

Sadly, it was during that visit that a malarial outbreak had taken the lives of both of Victoria's parents, causing Rebecca's parents to flee with their daughter back to England, leaving behind a sickly and contagious Victoria, who was not expected to survive.

Survive Victoria had, however, and no amount of across-the-sea cajoling had been successful in inducing her uncles to send her back to England to live with their sister, who thought it quite unsuitable for a young lady—particularly the only daughter of the Duke of Harrow—to be raised by three young bachelors. It was only now that Victoria had reached marriageable age that her mother's brothers had decided to relinquish their guardianship . . . a decision Victoria could not help noting coincided with her growing disgust for and complaints about their sometimes scandalous behavior. For example, she had never been able to get a single one of her uncles to refrain from putting his feet upon the table after a heavy meal.

Victoria could only dimly remember her own parents, and recalled the Gardiners just as vaguely. She had a distant memory of Rebecca joining her in a mud-pie-building contest. Now a golden-haired beauty of seventeen, Rebecca, Victoria could not help noticing, looked perfectly unlikely to take part in any such activity. She had not even deigned to join her family's undignified greeting of their cousin from India. Instead she'd stood a little apart, spinning a parasol in one hand and smiling rather coquettishly. It took a moment or two for Victoria to realize whom Rebecca was directing that smile toward, and when she did, she felt stunned. Why, it was none other than Captain Carstairs at whom Rebecca was smiling! And that gentleman, Victoria noticed with disgust, was smiling back! It was clear that the two of them had met before, because Victoria heard Rebecca call, over the din her younger brothers and sisters were making, "Good afternoon, Captain Carstairs!"

But though Captain Carstairs acknowledged the greeting with a deeper smile and a bow, he was not given a chance to reply, since Mrs. White began tugging rather forcefully on his sleeve. He bent down to hear what that good lady had to say, and Rebecca, looking a bit put out, finally glanced in Victoria's direction. It was then that Victoria saw her cousin smile again, revealing twin dimples on either side of her rosebud mouth.

"Welcome, Cousin Vicky," Rebecca said kindly.

Victoria found herself seized by a sudden wave of guilt. Just seconds before she had been struck by an inexplicable urge to box her pretty cousin's ears. And not because Becky had grown up to be so very beautiful. Victoria never envied other girls' looks, because while her own certainly might be lacking, she knew she had other qualities that made up for any want of dimples or curves.

No, Victoria had felt like slapping Rebecca because she'd caught her making eyes at Jacob Carstairs. Was the girl simple in the head? Did she not realize what a thoroughly despicable young man Jacob Carstairs was? And what was Victoria's aunt doing, allowing her daughter to be on friendly terms with such a reprobate?

Rebecca's "Welcome, Cousin Vicky," however, was all

that was civil and friendly. Victoria supposed she could forgive her. Besides, Victoria knew she would not have to put up with any of the Gardiners for very long. As soon as the earl returned from Lisbon, Victoria would demand that he procure a special license so that they could be married at once. A fortnight was all she thought she'd be able to bear of her aunt and uncle's hospitality.

Victoria smiled at her cousin, then turned her attention to thanking her aunt, whose long monologue concerning Victoria's defects had been interrupted by the sight of one of her younger children hauling a small dog about by the neck.

"Aunt Beatrice," Victoria began, "it's so lovely to see you again. Thank you so much for having me—"

"Jeremiah!" Mrs. Gardiner snapped. "Put that dog down! How many times have I told you not to hold him by the head? You might kill him!"

Not to be defeated in her attempt to thank her hosts, Victoria turned toward her uncle. "And it's very nice to see you again, too, Uncle Walter."

Her uncle, Mr. Gardiner, had terrified Victoria when she'd been little, due to his gruff uncommunicativeness. He had changed very little in the twelve years since she'd last seen him, she soon saw. "Harumph," was all he said to her, though he did manage a bow of acknowledgment. Then he turned toward Captain Carstairs, who stood a few feet away, and growled, "Welcome back, Carstairs.

And how did you find Africa?"

Victoria was not able to hear Mr. Carstairs's reply, because her aunt had started up again.

"Let's get poor Vicky home, darlings," she was braying for all the dockhands in London to hear. "She isn't used to English weather, and could easily come down with quinsy if the heavens break, which they seem threatening to do at any moment. And we wouldn't want Cousin Vicky with a red, sniffling nose, now, would we?" Mrs. Gardiner let out a laugh that Victoria was certain could be heard all the way back to Bombay. "'Twould frighten away all her suitors!"

Just as Victoria was certain she could not possibly feel more humiliated, she heard Jacob Carstairs quip, "Oh, I can think of one or two who wouldn't mind."

Victoria shot him an aggrieved look, but saw at once that it didn't do a bit of good. Captain Carstairs grinned at her above the heads of her cousins, and continued to do so as she was carried away by them toward the barouche. The last thing she saw, as they pulled away from the *Harmony*, was Mrs. White fluttering a lace handkerchief in her direction, crying, "Oh, good-bye, good-bye, Lady Victoria! I shall call upon you next week!" and beside her, Jacob Carstairs, smiling like a Hindi statue of Ginesh.

Insufferable man!

℧

CHAPTER THREE

"How lovely it must be to be rich," Rebecca Gardiner said with a sigh, as she held one of Victoria's many ball gowns to her shoulders and admired her reflection in the full-length looking glass of the dressing room they were to share during the course of Victoria's stay.

A stay that Victoria had already decided was going to be very short indeed. The Gardiners' London town house was quite nice, but with nine children—nine!—four dogs, three cats, assorted rabbits, ferrets, and budgies, two parents, a butler, cook, housekeeper, two maids, a nanny, a driver and a stableboy, the place was entirely too crowded for Victoria's taste. Already she was longing for the airy villa she and her uncles had shared, with a staff that lived out and only well-mannered dogs or the occasional mongoose—to kill the cobras that invariably coiled in the bath—as pets.

How very different things were in the Gardiner household! It seemed that Victoria could not turn around without stepping on a small child or cat's paw. As if that were not bad enough, the help left a good deal to be desired. Victoria could see that she was going to have to take her aunt's staff firmly in hand. She had already resolved that Mariah, the undermaid, was going to have to go. In fact, Victoria was too concerned over Mariah's less than careful unpacking of her belongings to pay much attention to what her cousin was saying.

"Yes," was how Victoria replied to her cousin's statement. To the hapless Mariah, however, who was crushing a very expensive crepe de chine wrapper, Victoria said, "That is to be hung, Mariah, not folded."

Rebecca, rather like Mariah, paid not the slightest bit of attention to Victoria.

"Mama says you've simply thousands of pounds." Rebecca pointed one of her toes, and admired the way it peeped out from the ruffled hem of the dress she held. "I wish *I* had thousands of pounds. If I did, I wouldn't stay *here* when I came to visit London. I would stay in a hotel, and order ices to be brought to me all day long."

"If you ate ices all day, you would become ill. Besides, my uncles wouldn't let me stay in a hotel," Victoria said. "They said it wasn't considered proper in England for a young lady to stay in a hotel without a suitable chaperon. Although in India no one would think twice about it."

"It must be divine," Rebecca said, clearly not in the least interested in hearing about India, "to have all the money in the world to buy pretty things. Tell me, how many fans do you own?"

"Oh, dozens," Victoria said. "It was so hot most of the year in Jaipur. Oh, Mariah, *do* be careful with that gown. Can't you see it's silk?"

"I only have two fans," Rebecca said glumly. "And Jeremiah ripped one of them. Oh, it isn't fair! You have all the luck—a fortune, dozens of fans, and delicious Captain Carstairs all to yourself for weeks and weeks."

That got Victoria's full attention, as nothing else her cousin had said had. Mariah and her slipshod unpacking skills were forgotten as Victoria spun around to stare at Rebecca.

"Captain *Carstairs?*" she cried in astonishment.

Rebecca nodded dreamily to her reflection in the long mirror. "Isn't he wonderful? I wish Papa had left me behind in India with you back in 'ninety-eight. Then you and I might have sailed back to England together, and had the company of delicious Mr. Carstairs morning, noon, and night."

Victoria made a retching noise. It wasn't ladylike, but she couldn't help it.

Rebecca noticed, and raised both her eyebrows in surprise.

"You didn't enjoy Captain Carstairs's company during the voyage?" she asked in incredulous tones.

"Hardly!" Victoria declared. "Jacob Carstairs is the most contrary gentleman I have ever had the displeasure of meeting!"

Rebecca looked shocked. "But he is so exceedingly amiable," she said.

Victoria snorted. "Exceedingly rude, impertinent, and offensive, you mean. And if you dare to tell me that he is considered by the *ton* to be anything like a catch, I shall scream."

"Well, he is," Rebecca said bluntly, and Victoria obliged her by screaming, shrilly enough to cause the ham-handed Mariah nearly to drop the bottle of rose attar she'd been lifting from one of Victoria's many trunks.

"But Captain Carstairs is all that is gentlemanly," Rebecca went on very seriously. "He has business dealings with Papa and frequently stays to dinner—and often invites us, in return, to dine with him and his mother—so we are fortunate enough to see him quite often. He has never been anything but charming. And he is so excessively handsome and droll. And quite wealthy, besides."

"Wealthy?" Victoria, rescuing the rose attar, looked doubtful. "He's only a naval officer."

"Not at all," Rebecca said. "Do you know that ship you sailed, the *Harmony*? Well, Jacob Carstairs owns it. He owns the entire Harmony line. It was his father's company, but when he died it all went to Captain Carstairs. And he, in a few short years, turned it from what was at the time of his father's death—a bit of a disappointment, I think—into the quite profitable company it is today. Jacob Carstairs, thanks to his hard work, is quite fantastically rich."

Victoria digested this. Jacob Carstairs, fantastically rich? Well, that certainly explained why he'd seemed to feel no compunction about teasing a duke's daughter.

Still, what about those collar points?

"I don't believe it," Victoria said finally.

"Believe it," Rebecca said. "He has forty or fifty thousand pounds, at least. He is every bit as wealthy as you are, Vicky."

Victoria sent her cousin a pained look. "Must you call me that?" she asked.

"Vicky?" Rebecca looked mildly startled. "But we've always called you Vicky."

"It's *Victoria*," Victoria said. "Vicky is a child's name. And I am no longer a child. I am, in fact, very nearly a married woman."

She slid her gaze toward her cousin to see how she took this news. She was gratified to see an astonished Rebecca suck in her breath.

"What?" Rebecca cried. "You're engaged?"

"Indeed I am," Victoria said, delighted that she was able to share her news at last. She'd been feeling as if she might burst from keeping it to herself. It was a relief to tell someone, even if that someone had the ill judgment to think of Jacob Carstairs as marriageable.

"See, here is his signet ring." Victoria held out her hand so that Rebecca could examine the gold ring that Victoria was forced to wear on her middle finger, and not her third, as it was so large on her. Mariah, sidling by with her arms full of Victoria's underthings, also stopped to admire it.

"But this is the crest of the Earl of Malfrey," Rebecca cried as she bent to examine the ring. "Oh, Vicky! Don't say you are engaged to Hugo Rothschild!"

"Indeed I am," Victoria said importantly, pleased to see that this news seemed to be causing Mariah to treat her pantaloons with more reverence. "I met him on board the ship, and he asked me to marry him three nights ago, just before he disembarked for Lisbon, where he has business." Then she added as an afterthought, "You must promise not to tell anyone, Becky. You, too, Mariah. Lord Malfrey asked that we keep our engagement secret until he returns to London and can introduce me properly to his mother."

"I'll not say a word, m'lady," Mariah declared staunchly. Rebecca was not so quick to promise, however.

"Engaged!" Rebecca looked stunned. "And to Lord Malfrey! He is so very handsome! And stylish, too. Why, I have seen him at Almack's many a time, and never once has he worn the same waistcoat. He is a most pleasing gentleman . . . all that is amiable and obliging." Then the pretty face clouded over. "But Vicky, you're only sixteen. Will your uncles allow you to marry so young?"

Victoria shrugged. "What can they do about it? They're back in India, and I'm here."

"There is quite a lot they could do about it," Rebecca declared. "They could refuse to allow it. And then you'd have to elope. But then they might cut you off! And then what would the two of you live on? For I have heard, Vicky, that the earl's fortune is not what it once was."

Victoria said kindly, "Don't trouble yourself on that account, Becky. My uncles cannot cut me off, for I came into my fortune last year. The money my father left for me is mine to do with what I like. And I know all about Lord Malfrey's lack of wealth. That's why our engagement is such a joy to me. I've always longed for something worthy to do with my wealth." Victoria tried to put from her head the uncomfortable memory of Jacob Carstairs saying earlier that day, *Well, you must be feeling very happy indeed, Miss Bee. Finally a chance to be useful to someone.* Such a tiresome young man! "Now I will be able to put my fortune to good use, helping to restore my husband's family to its former place as one of the best of London."

Rebecca continued to look dubious. "I don't think Mama will like it, Vicky," she said. "Nor Papa, for that matter. In fact, I think it might be my duty as your elder cousin to tell them. You are *so* young, you know."

Victoria prickled. "Only a year younger than you," she pointed out.

"Still," Rebecca said gravely. "There's a great difference between sixteen and seventeen, you know. After all, I've already had a season out, and you haven't. What could you possibly know about men? You've spent the whole of your life in India!"

Living with three of the most vexing, egotistical men in the world, who were completely incapable of taking their boot heels off the tabletop, Victoria thought crossly to herself. *What I don't know about men, Miss Becky, would fit into your thimble with room to spare.*

"Are you saying you don't think Lord Malfrey will make me a good husband?" was what she asked aloud.

"Oh, no," Rebecca said. "Not at all. Only that . . . well, can you really be so sure you love him, Vicky, at only sixteen?"

Victoria, annoyed, asked, "Can you really be so sure you love Captain Carstairs at only seventeen?"

Rebecca blushed prettily. "I did not say I loved him."

"Well, you do an excellent imitation of it. 'He is so handsome and charming and droll,' were your words, I believe."

Rebecca tossed her head until her golden curls bounced. "What if I do love him? At least Jacob Carstairs made his own fortune, and won't need to depend on his wife to pay his tailor's bills."

As there was nothing Victoria could say in response to the first part of her cousin's remark, she responded only to the second half: "Captain Carstairs might think about switching tailors," Victoria snapped, "as his own is allowing him to gad about town in scandalously low collar points."

Rebecca sucked in her breath. "There is nothing wrong with Mr. Carstairs's collar points!"

It was on the tip of Victoria's tongue to assert that Jacob Carstairs's collar points were as low as her opinion of his character, when it occurred to her that it would not do to alienate her cousin. Victoria had plans for Rebecca. For no sooner had she seen her cousin standing on the dock making eyes at Jacob Carstairs than Victoria had decided that he was the last man in the world with whom she could allow her cousin to become involved. Victoria intended to find a friend of Lord Malfrey's for Rebecca, so that the four of them could summer together at the earl's estate in the lake district. It was Victoria's duty, she knew, to rescue Rebecca not only from the obnoxious company of her entirely too large family, but from Jacob Carstairs, as well.

And so Victoria swallowed down her ire and said in the sweetest voice imaginable, "Of course there's nothing wrong with Captain Carstairs's collar points. I was only teasing. Let's not quarrel, Becky."

Rebecca did not look inclined to stop quarreling. Nor, it turned out, did she seem inclined to keep her mouth shut on the subject of Victoria's engagement.

"It just feels wrong," she said, "hiding something like this from Mama."

Victoria glanced at the gown Mariah happened to be unfolding from the last of her trunks.

"You know," Victoria said slyly, "I probably won't be staying long beneath your father's roof, Becky. Soon Lord

Malfrey and I will marry, and I'll go away to live with him. Which is too bad, because I was just thinking what fun it was going to be, living with another woman. I've never done it, you know . . . not since my mother died. I was thinking what a jolly time we'll have, staying up late gossiping, and trying on each other's clothes. If you like something of mine, you know, you need only ask to borrow it, and it's yours for as long as you like. That gown you were admiring in the mirror, for instance. Wouldn't you like to wear it to dinner tonight?"

In half a second, Rebecca's expression turned from mulish to wistful.

"That gown?" she said. "I really might wear it? You wouldn't mind?"

"Not at all," Victoria said. "But you'll need to take the fan that goes with it. It's the blue feathered one, Mariah, the one you just put in the top drawer."

Mariah pulled out the aforementioned fan and presented it to Rebecca with a curtsy. "'Twill go with your eyes, miss," she said obsequiously. And Victoria began to sense that there might be some hope for Mariah after all.

And hope for Rebecca as well, Victoria decided later, when, garbed in borrowed finery, her cousin made quite a splash as she entered the dining room. Mrs. Gardiner, fearing—wrongly, of course—that Victoria would be too fatigued from her long sea voyage to wish to go out her first night in London, had arranged for a quiet family dinner—though Mrs. Gardiner's idea of quiet and Victoria's contrasted sharply. Quiet, to Victoria, meant shutting all the little Gardiners up in their nursery so that the adults might eat in relative peace.

Quiet to Mrs. Gardiner, however, appeared simply to mean that no outside guests had been invited to dine with the family.

And so when Victoria and Rebecca, summoned by Perkins, the butler, appeared in the dining room, it was to observe young Annabelle and Judith leading their younger brothers in a mad dash around the table, Elizabeth swinging from the portieres, and Jeremiah dragging an unfortunate kitten about by the scruff of its neck with his teeth, in an apparent imitation of "Kitty." It was a testament to Rebecca's beauty—or perhaps to Victoria's dressmaker back in Jaipur—that the sight of their sister in the borrowed blue gown caused all such activity to cease. Jeremiah even dropped the kitten, who scampered, with much foresight for so young a creature, up the portieres, and thus out of reach of her pint-sized tormentor.

"Becky!" cried Clara, who was closest to Rebecca in age, being fourteen and very aware of the fact that she was well on her way to being as pretty as her elder sister. "You look like a princess!"

Mr. Gardiner said nothing except, "What, tureen of beef again?" after a glance into the chafing dish, but Mrs. Gardiner was full of compliments for her daughter.

"Such a lovely gown!" she cried. "It goes so well with your eyes, my dear. It is very generous of your cousin to loan it to you. It might look well, if dear Vicky will loan it to you again, at Dame Ashforth's cotillion next week. Take care not to spill anything on it tonight and ruin it."

"I won't, Mama," Rebecca murmured demurely, and Victoria knew that her secret—the one concerning her engagement—was safe. She was feeling very smug—though not at all pleased with the Gardiners' cook, who seemed to put very little actual beef in her tureen of beef. Victoria saw at once that she and Cook were going to have to have words—when Perkins appeared in the doorway and announced, "Captain Carstairs."

Victoria very nearly dropped her spoon. Captain Carstairs? *Captain Carstairs?* Hadn't she just left him—with hopes that it would be forever—at the docks? What on earth was he doing here, at her aunt and uncle's house, just a few hours later?

"Hmmph," her uncle said, not doing at all a tidy job with his napkin. Bits of tureen clung to his beard. "Show him in, show him in."

"Oh, yes, do," Mrs. Gardiner, from the other end of the table, cried. "And set another place at the table, Perkins. The captain will want to join us, I'm sure."

"Hurrah," cried Jeremiah, upsetting his bowl with a stray elbow. "Uncle Jacob is here!"

Uncle Jacob? Victoria could not imagine that her

evening could get any worse. Was she never to be free of
the company of this obnoxious young man?

A few seconds later he appeared in the doorway in a
fresh waistcoat and shirt, his boots highly shined as ever . . .
but his collar points still at least two inches lower than they
ought to have been. The children—a clearly undisciplined
brood—leaped from their seats at the sight of him, and
surged forward in a wall of beaming faces and beef-tureeny
hands, crying, "Uncle Jacob! Uncle Jacob!"

Captain Carstairs managed quickly to extricate himself,
however, by producing a bag and declaring, "Yes, it's me.
It's good to see all of you again. And look what I've
brought you from Africa!"

The children left off clinging to his coat and fell
upon the bag instead, like a pack of ravenous little
vultures. *Clever of him!* Victoria could not help thinking,
and wished she had had such a bag back upon the pier,
with which she might have defended herself against the
Gardiner horde. Jacob Carstairs, free at last, turned his
bright-eyed gaze upon the four adults left at the table—
five if you counted Clara, who had evidently decided
herself too old to leap upon the bag like her younger
siblings, but who nevertheless was eyeing it with undis-
guised curiosity.

"Good evening," the young captain said, bowing politely
toward Mrs. Gardiner, Rebecca, and Victoria. "So sorry to
interrupt your dinner. It was good of you to invite me in."

"Nonsense," Mr. Gardiner said gruffly. "Sit down and eat."

"Yes, do, Jacob," Mrs. Gardiner beseeched him. "That is, if your mother can spare you. I don't want her to be put out with me, stealing you away your first night back in town after so long a voyage."

"My mother has gone to the opera," Captain Carstairs said. "She did not know I was to arrive today, and did not feel she could give up such fine seats."

"Then you are orphaned for the night!" Mrs. Gardiner cried. "And so it is my duty to feed you! Sit, sit, do. There is plenty for everyone."

"In that case"——Mr. Carstairs dropped into the chair that Perkins had placed at the table for him——"I shall be happy to. There is nothing I enjoy better, as I'm sure you know, Mrs. Gardiner, than your fine cook's excellent tureen of beef."

Victoria shot the young captain a look of complete incredulity over her own bowl of the watery stuff. She had always thought there was something a little off about Jacob Carstairs, but now she began to feel that perhaps he was actually mad. He was either mad or he was dissembling, because there was nothing in the least bit excellent about the Gardiners' cook's tureen of beef.

Then Jacob Carstairs did something that confirmed Victoria's belief that he was not wholly sound in the head. He winked at her! Across the dining table!

She was certain he winked only because he knew

as well as she did that the tureen of beef was terrible. Unfortunately, however, Rebecca caught the wink and misinterpreted it, flinging Victoria an accusing look. As if, after everything Victoria had said upstairs, there was the slightest chance she had designs on Jacob Carstairs!

If Captain Carstairs noticed Rebecca's hostile glance in Victoria's direction, he did not indicate it. Instead he said to the older girl, "Miss Gardiner, that's a lovely gown you have on this evening. I don't believe I've ever seen it on you before."

Rebecca seemed instantly to forget her antipathy toward Victoria, and simpered in the young captain's direction. "Why, thank you, Captain."

"It's not hers," young Jeremiah announced from the floor, where he and his brothers and sisters sat, sorting through the items they'd found at the bottom of the bag Captain Carstairs had dropped, which included, if their appreciative cries were to be believed, shrunken heads and monkey's paws, though Victoria highly doubted an actual shrunken head would have been allowed through customs. "It's Cousin Vicky's."

Rebecca instantly turned a deep shade of umber, and Victoria uttered a quick and silent prayer of thanks to the Lord for taking her parents before they'd had a chance to provide her with siblings.

"Ah," Captain Carstairs said. "I see. Cousin Vicky's. And I trust Cousin Vicky is finding London to her liking?"

Victoria longed to dash her tureen of beef in the handsome young man's lap. Instead she merely said, "It's been tolerable—thus far," and hoped he took the *thus far* to mean up until his arrival at the Gardiners' dinner table, which was precisely how she'd intended it.

If Captain Carstairs got her meaning, however, he gave no indication. Instead he picked up the glass of madeira that Perkins had poured for him, and raised it in Victoria's direction.

"I'd like to declare a toast," he said. "To the charming Lady Victoria."

"Hear, hear," cried Mrs. Gardiner, raising her glass as well. "We are so delighted to have you back in England at last, my child. It's been too, too long."

Mr. Gardiner said nothing but "Harumph," and lowered his glass again.

But young Captain Carstairs was not finished.

"May she take London society by storm," he went on, still gazing steadily at Victoria, who, with a sudden sinking feeling, narrowed her eyes at him in warning. It was a warning, however, that the young man did not heed. "And not forget us when she is, as I understand she is soon to become, the new Lady Malfrey."

CHAPTER FOUR

"You did it on purpose," Victoria said accusingly.

"I swear I didn't," Captain Carstairs said with a careless laugh that infuriated her all the more.

"Don't swear," Victoria said with a sniff. "It isn't polite."

"Well, then, I *promise* you I didn't."

Jacob Carstairs was looking infuriatingly cool and collected. How dared he look so calm, when Victoria was simmering over with anger at him?

Well, he wouldn't look half so cocksure by the time Victoria was through with him. It had been remarkably stupid of him to ask her to dance, knowing full well that she was still put out with him for revealing her secret engagement to her aunt and uncle. Perhaps he'd thought because a full week had gone by since the incident, that her ire might be at its ebb. *Foolish man!* Victoria had once managed to stay angry at her uncle Henry for a full a month, and *that* had been only because he'd used one of her best shawls to wipe down his pistols after a duel.

Captain Carstairs, on the other hand, had ruined Victoria's life.

This was not, Victoria felt, an exaggeration, either. Since his thoughtless announcement that night at dinner, Victoria's existence had turned into a living nightmare. Her aunt would not leave her alone on the subject of her engagement. Every time Victoria turned around, it seemed, all she heard was Lord Malfrey this, and Lord Malfrey that. How Victoria wished Lord Malfrey would hurry up and get home from Lisbon, so that she might appeal to him to have a word with her relations—or at the very least, convince him to elope at once, and remove her from their company forever. For they were driving her to distraction with their petty admonishments and concerns.

What business was it of theirs anyway whom she chose to marry? If she wanted to marry an Indian fakir, who were they to try to stop her? For heaven's sake, her uncles had sent her to England with instructions to find a husband. Well, she'd found one . . . and a more exemplary groom simply did not exist. Lord Malfrey was everything that was gentlemanly and admirable—intelligent, polite, attentive, and very, very handsome.

So what was the problem?

"You've only known each other a few months," was Victoria's aunt's lament. But a few months was a great deal longer than many couples knew each other before taking their vows. Why, in India, more often than not a bride did not even meet her husband to be until their wedding day!

And here Victoria had spent three whole months at sea getting to know hers! No, "You've only known each other a few months" was no sort of argument.

Her aunt, Victoria knew, was only put out because Victoria had managed to get a husband before Rebecca had. Which wasn't entirely fair, because Rebecca had only her pretty face to recommend her, and no fortune to speak of. Victoria was perfectly aware that a part of Lord Malfrey's attraction to her was her inheritance. She did not blame him for it. Men had to eat, too, same as women.

But she also knew that, had she been horse-faced or even, God forbid, redheaded, Lord Malfrey would not have taken the time to learn of her fortune. He would have dismissed her out of hand. No, her money made things easier, certainly, but it was her person first, and *then* her purse, that Hugo Rothschild had found so attractive.

But what was so very wrong with that? What was a marriage if not a business transaction? Victoria could not help thinking that the Indian way of courtship and marriage made more sense than the way the English went about it. In India parents decided, often at birth, whom their children would marry. When the boy and girl came of age, certain transactions ensued, generally involving goods of some sort. Some girls were worth many goods, some only a few. After these transactions, the couple was joined in holy matrimony, and everyone went home with their allotted goods, and that was that.

In England, it was entirely more complicated. No marital arrangements were made on the part of the children's parents at all. Instead, mothers and fathers kept their daughters tucked out of sight until their sixteenth or seventeenth birthdays, at which point they were suddenly pushed into society—something Victoria had learned was called a girl's "coming out," or "first season"—and paraded in front of the marriageable bachelors who happened to be in town and not back at their country estates, still shooting grouse, as they'd been doing all winter. The single men then decided which of these many girls they liked, and then from there, which girl had the largest dowry.

The English style of courtship seemed perfectly barbaric—and unfair to the girls, Victoria felt. For what if a girl were not attractive, or poor? Who would want to marry her then? Perhaps the worst part of the English courtship rituals, Victoria learned soon after her arrival on English soil, was something called Almack's. It was nothing more than a series of large rooms in which everyone who was anyone in London society gathered every Wednesday night in order to dance and show off their new spring wardrobe. Almack's was, to Victoria, a nightmarish crush of humanity. It made her long for the airy and open market squares of Jaipur, which held occasional festivals, when it was not monsoon season, at which everyone from neighboring villages showed up. How she missed the sparkling saris, the fire-eaters, the highly spiced savories!

There was nothing comparable at Almack's. Bland punch, stale biscuits, and even staler conversation. There were no fire-eaters, and not even a single elephant.

The utter lack of other diversion made the presence of Jacob Carstairs surprisingly welcome. He did not, according to her cousin Rebecca, come often to Almack's. But upon Victoria's first visit to the place, there he was, looking very well in evening dress, though his collar points were still distressingly low—the lowest in the room, in fact. Victoria had thrown her cousin a significant look upon noticing them, as if to say, *See? What was I telling you? No respect for fashion whatsoever.*

Still, unfashionable collar points or not, Captain Carstairs greeted both girls very cordially, and asked each of them for a dance—to Rebecca's delight, and Victoria's disgust. If Jacob Carstairs thought that she was going to meekly forget the humiliation he'd put her through the week before, he was in for a rude shock.

"You knew I hadn't yet told my aunt and uncle about my engagement to Lord Malfrey," Victoria said as Jacob Carstairs took her hand for the dance she'd promised him. "Admit it. You were hoping to cause a scene."

"Which I did," Captain Carstairs said, not even attempting to hide his happy smile at the memory of Victoria's aunt falling into a swoon and her daughters' attempts to revive her. Victoria's uncle's reaction had not been nearly as satisfying. He had merely called for Perkins to bring him a whiskey.

"Well, I don't think it's anything to be proud of," Victoria said severely. "You put the entire house into an uproar."

"*I* didn't," Jacob said. "*You're* the one who wanted to marry a man your family doesn't approve of, not me. I just informed them of the fact. It doesn't do any good to kill the messenger."

"My family doesn't disapprove of Lord Malfrey," Victoria informed him. "It's my marrying so soon after my arrival that they don't like. Not that there's anything they can do about it."

Jacob lifted a single dark brow. "Isn't there?"

Victoria gave a haughty toss of her head. "Hardly! What can they do? They don't hold my purse strings; I do. I can do as I like."

"And what you like," Jacob said, "is to marry Hugo Rothschild. A man you hardly know."

"Why does everyone keep saying that?" Victoria shook her head in wonder. "I know him very well indeed. I was with him for a month longer than I was with you on the *Harmony*, you'll remember."

"As if I could forget," Jacob said obliquely. Then he demanded, "And just what was Lord Malfrey, a gentleman whom I understand is in some financial straits, doing in Bombay, anyway? Did you ever bother asking him that?"

"Of course I did," Victoria said. "Lord Malfrey was seeing to the sale of some property left to him by a distant relation."

"In *India?*"

"That's correct." Victoria wondered why she was bothering to explain her fiancé's business affairs to this man, who was not even a relation, but seemed to harbor some sort of absurd proprietary feelings toward her just the same. "And now he's off to Lisbon to spend the proceeds buying back some family portraits that he was forced to part with a few years ago, when he was in somewhat different financial straits."

Jacob Carstairs looked disgusted. "Good Lord," he said. "And you really want to marry this fellow? It seems he can barely manage to keep his personal affairs in order."

"Of course he can't," Victoria said. "That's why he needs me."

"To pay his bills, you mean," Jacob said, rudely.

"To help him organize his life," Victoria corrected him.

But she instantly regretted her unguarded words when Jacob Carstairs let out a bark of laughter, and cried, "Good Lord, I'd almost forgotten. Of course a fellow like that would appeal to a busy bee like you. Why, he needs no end of improving."

Victoria leveled a very meaningful gaze at Jacob Carstairs's collar points and said, "I can think of a few things I'd like to improve about *you.*"

"It all makes sense now." Jacob did not seem to have noticed the direction of her gaze, nor heard her remark. "The Hugo Rothschilds of the world are irresistible to all little Miss Bees like you. Tell me, where did you intend to start with him? His finances, of course, are in lamentable condition. But if I were you, I'd begin with his mother. I understand she's quite a gorgon."

"I'll tell you where I'd start with you," Victoria piped up. "You need to learn to keep your—"

"Ah, no," Jacob said, lifting a warning finger. "You and I are not engaged. I have not paid for the privilege of one of your improving speeches—elucidating as I am sure they must be. You will have to save your lectures for me until such time as you are unattached again."

"Well," Victoria said, feeling more vexed with him than ever, "then you will have to wait forever, for I plan never to be unattached again."

Jacob, though the dance abruptly finished, forgot to bow in response to Victoria's curtsy. Instead he just stood there looking down at her with a very astonished expression on his face.

"What?" he said, seemingly quite unaware that all the other couples save themselves were moving from the dance floor. "You still intend to go through with it?"

"With what?" Victoria thought that, for all he was in charge of a shipping line worth many thousands of pounds, Jacob Carstairs was rather dim. "My wedding to

Lord Malfrey? Why, certainly. I think I already informed you of that."

"But . . . but your aunt and uncle," Jacob stammered. "I saw the way they reacted to the news. Surely they can't . . . they haven't given you permission to wed him."

"Of course they haven't." Really, but Victoria almost felt sorry for Jacob Carstairs. He was not taking the information that his little scheme of ruining her future had failed at all well. Victoria, herself a habitual schemer, had learned to take her own foiled plots in stride. "But I don't need their permission to marry. I am of age, and can do as I like. They don't approve, but they can't stop me."

"Then you are still engaged to him?" Jacob demanded. "And intend to remain so?"

"Indeed," Victoria said. "Why shouldn't I?"

"Because Hugo Rothschild," Jacob Carstairs blurted, "is a rogue!"

Slander! Victoria had never heard such a blatant lie in her life. And she doubted that Almack's had ever played host to such libel, as well, at least if the way everyone was staring at them as they stood nose-to-nose—well, Victoria's nose to the captain's chest, to be perfectly truthful—in the center of the room was any indication.

"A rogue!" Victoria echoed scathingly. "I like that! If that's true, what, pray, do you call yourself, Captain?"

"A concerned friend," Jacob replied from between gritted teeth.

"Ha!" Victoria laughed in his face. "And what kind of friend, Captain Carstairs, goes about trying to destroy another person's one chance at happiness?"

"If Hugo Rothschild is your one chance at happiness," Jacob said in a snarl, "then I'm a hurdygurdy man!"

Victoria narrowed her eyes at him. "In that case, your monkey seems to be missing," she informed him.

"This," Jacob Carstairs said, suddenly turning away from her and striding from the dance floor, "is intolerable. Where is your uncle?"

Victoria, aware of all the stares they were attracting, hurried after the captain, having to run a little in order to keep up with his long, manly strides.

"What do you want my uncle for?" she asked curiously. "I already told you, he can't stop me from marrying whom I like."

"Ha," Jacob Carstairs said with a certain amount of scorn. "We'll see about that."

Very interested in this turn of events, Victoria trailed after him, not noticing that Rebecca was tagging along as well until she heard her call her name.

"Vicky!"

Victoria turned her head and saw Rebecca tripping along beside her.

"Oh," Victoria said. "Hello."

"What is happening?" Rebecca wanted to know. "What were you and the captain arguing about out on the dance floor? Everyone was looking! I was so embarrassed for you."

"Just Lord Malfrey," Victoria informed her cousin with a shrug.

"Lord Malfrey?" Rebecca, resplendent in another gown she'd borrowed from Victoria, looked more beautiful than ever, in spite of the wilting heat of the crowded room. "Oh, dear. Captain Carstairs dislikes him so."

"I know it," Victoria said. "He is going to have words with your father. He thinks there is something Uncle Walter can do to prevent my marrying Hugo."

Rebecca reached out to grip Victoria's arm, keeping her from flying after the agitated young ship captain.

"He *what?*" Rebecca demanded rather loudly.

"He thinks he can stop me from marrying Lord Malfrey," Victoria explained. Heavens, but her cousin was slow to understand the simplest things sometimes. "Come along, Becky. If we don't hurry, we'll miss all the fun!"

"Fun!" Rebecca looked as stunned as if Victoria had pinched her. "Is that what you think it is? *Fun?*"

Victoria, eager as she was not to miss a moment of what promised to be an amusing spectacle—Captain Carstairs rebuking her uncle, that is—could not help but notice a spark of anger in her cousin's blue eyes.

"Why, Becky," she said, wondering what on earth could have upset her cousin now. For Rebecca, Victoria had discovered during her weeklong sojourn with the

Gardiners, had a volatile temper, and was somewhat prone to dramatics. "Whatever is the matter?"

"Isn't it obvious?" Rebecca snapped.

Victoria could only ascertain, from the high color in the other girl's face, that she was in some sort of physical discomfort. Accordingly, Victoria asked solicitously, "Are your stays too tight? I warned Mariah——"

"No!" Rebecca grew even more red-faced at the mention of her corset. "Good heavens, Vicky, are you completely dense? Can't you see what's happening?"

Victoria blinked. "I guess not," she said. "I suppose you'd better tell me."

Rebecca stamped a slippered foot. "Oh, you are the most infuriating girl! Can't you see? He's in love with you!"

Victoria blinked some more. "Who is?"

"Captain Carstairs!"

CHAPTER FIVE

Victoria let out a merry laugh.

"Oh, Becky," she cried. "You *are* droll. Stop joking now, and let's go watch the captain and your father. It's sure to be diverting."

"I'm *not* joking," Rebecca said, tightening her fingers on Victoria's arm so that her grip actually began to hurt. "Captain Carstairs is in love with you!"

"Becky." Victoria, seeing now that her cousin was perfectly serious, tried her best not to smile. It wouldn't do, she knew, to laugh too hard at Rebecca, who was a serious sort of girl. Still, it *was* amusing. The idea of Captain Carstairs, who could never seem to look at Victoria without seeing—and then commenting upon—a fault, being in love with her! *La, what a joke!*

What wasn't a joke, however, was how Becky seemed to feel. The older girl was angry—really angry—and Victoria supposed she couldn't blame her. The captain's behavior *was* infuriating . . . especially because it was so peculiar. Jacob Carstairs didn't care for her a jot.

But Victoria supposed she could see how Becky might misinterpret his motivation. Which only made her more convinced than ever that she needed to find a gentleman more deserving of her cousin's ardor than the horrid Jacob Carstairs.

"Captain Carstairs is hardly in love with me," Victoria explained patiently. "If anything he despises me, and has made his contempt perfectly well known."

"If he isn't in love with you, why does he care so much about whether or not you marry?" Rebecca wanted to know.

"Captain Carstairs doesn't care whether or not I marry," Victoria replied as calmly as she could. Really, but romantic, imaginative girls like Rebecca were such a lot of work. Victoria was quite glad she had no imagination to speak of, and could turn her mind to practical things, like financial planning and household management. "He just doesn't want me to marry Lord Malfrey."

"Because he's jealous!"

"Because Captain Carstairs has some sort of absurd prejudice against Lord Malfrey," Victoria said. "I don't know why. It has something to do with poor Lord Malfrey not having any money. He went so far as to call him a rogue."

Rebecca looked suitably shocked. "He didn't!"

"He did. Which, if that isn't the pot calling the kettle black, I don't know what is."

"Oh, Vicky," Rebecca said, her blue eyes wide as forget-me-nots. "Captain Carstairs is as far from being a rogue as . . . well, as Papa is!"

"Suit yourself," Victoria said, unwilling to raise her cousin's ire any more than it already was by strenuously disagreeing, as she would have liked to. Really, but she would have to find a nice young man, and soon, for Becky to fall in love with, or she would never hear the end of Captain Carstairs. "Honestly, Becky, you really needn't bother your head about Captain Carstairs and me. We are quite thorough enemies. Why, I believe he hates me every bit as much as I hate him."

This mollified Rebecca only slightly.

"It does *seem* as if he hates you," she admitted grudgingly, "the way he is always criticizing you. Like last week at dinner, when he laughed at your idea that women should be allowed to run military operations from Whitehall."

"There," Victoria said, though she did not find that memory quite as comforting as Rebecca evidently did. She quite fancied that, if only the British Empire would recognize her superior organizational skills, she could handily settle a half dozen of its most pressing foreign conflicts by teatime. Still, she stifled her protest and said, "You see? If he were in love with me, would he have laughed quite so hard?"

"No," Rebecca admitted. "And I once heard the captain telling Mama that he prefers quiet, sensitive girls like me. Everyone knows *you* aren't in the least sensitive."

Victoria, who thought that *sensitive* was really just a polite way to describe girls who were incapable of taking care of themselves, was not surprised to hear that the captain liked young ladies of this particular bent. He seemed the type of fellow to prefer a girl who fainted at the sight of blood, as Victoria was certain Rebecca would, to one who would calmly stanch its flow with a pocket handkerchief, as Victoria had done the time her uncle Jasper accidentally ran his bayonet through his big toe.

"Er," she said. "Yes. So don't you see, Becky? Captain Carstairs can't possibly be in love with me."

"But if that's so," Rebecca said with a final suspicious glance, "why is he always looking at you? Because he is, Vicky. Whenever he thinks you aren't looking he stares and stares. He did it at supper, and he's been doing it here all night long. Even when he was dancing with me, he kept looking across the room at you!"

Victoria laid a comforting hand upon her cousin's puffed sleeve.

"Of course he did," she said kindly. "Because he's wondering how on earth two cousins could be more different. I'm sure he's looking at me and asking himself, 'Now why can't Lady Victoria be more like her pretty cousin Miss Gardiner? Miss Gardiner would never allow her perfect china-white skin to get so brown in the sun. Miss Gardiner would never tell her maid that if she caught her folding instead of hanging her silk gowns again, she'd dismiss her. Miss Gardiner would never reduce Cook to tears with her scathing indictment of her tureen of beef.'"

Rebecca's scowl brightened. "Goodness, I never thought of it like that. You're quite right, Vicky. Captain Carstairs couldn't possibly be in love with you. You are so very interfering."

This wasn't entirely what Victoria wanted to hear, but at least her cousin had stopped glaring so balefully at her, which was a definite relief. "Champion," Victoria said. "Now let's go see what your father says when Jacob Carstairs asks him why he hasn't forbidden me from marrying Lord Malfrey."

Though Rebecca put up a token resistance—it wasn't right, she said, to spy upon gentlemen, particularly her own father—Victoria managed eventually to drag her across the room, causing quite a stir and no small amount of headshaking from the gallery of matrons who observed this unorthodox behavior in the hallowed rooms of Almack's. The general opinion of the matrons—and throughout London—seemed to be that Lady Victoria Arbuthnot was rather a handful. The majority of the society matrons felt quite sorry for Beatrice Gardiner, who'd been put in charge of the headstrong girl.

But at the same time they couldn't help rather envying Rebecca's mother, because Victoria's handling of the Gardiners' cook had already become the stuff of legend. The description of Victoria's ashen complexion when presented with tureen of beef a second night in a row had made its way through London's finest kitchens, eventually trickling upstairs from the servants' quarters and into the boudoirs of Mayfair's finest hostesses. Her quiet request to be excused, her subsequent trip through the baize door and down to the kitchen, her polite but firm instructions to the Gardiners' cook that never—*never*—was she to serve tureen of beef in that household again, or she would be made to suffer the consequences, had caused many a cook who had for years terrorized her employers with threats to quit if her food was criticized to quake with terror. Already the warning had been passed from cook to cook throughout the land: only those with a stout heart and a steady hand with a basting brush need apply for work in the household of the new Lady Malfrey.

No one blamed Beatrice, of course, for her niece's reputation. The young lady was an orphan, after all, and had had the misfortune of having been raised in India like a little heathen, since for all intents and purposes, her uncles had ignored her until she grew too strident in her criticism of them for them not to pay attention. Then they had promptly shipped her off for their poor sister to deal with. Such a pity, too, because her dearly departed mother had been such a great beauty, such a gentle creature . . . so gentle, in fact, that she was quite hopeless with the help. . . .

Sadly, Jacob's speech was just winding down as Victoria and her cousin approached.

"At best, sir, your niece will be dragged down to his level," the captain was pontificating. "At worst, her reputation will be ruined, and she won't be able to show her face in a single decent household in all of London."

Victoria bitterly regretted having missed the beginning of this speech. It sounded quite a good one.

"Er," Rebecca's father was heard to reply. "Um. Ah."

"Show some spirit, Uncle Gardiner," Victoria urged him, with enthusiasm. "Tell him to save his breath to cool his porridge."

But her uncle only turned very red in the face, muttered something about going in search of punch, and departed. Jacob Carstairs turned on Victoria with blazing eyes—really blazing, the way a tiger's eyes blazed just as it was set to pounce—and said in a very deep and commanding voice, "If your family won't do anything to keep you from making this excessively foolish match, Lady Victoria, I can assure you I will."

"Oh, Captain Carstairs," Rebecca said, batting her eyelashes worshipfully at the young captain. Really, but Victoria was going to have to put an end to this absurd fixation of her cousin's very soon indeed. "It is so kind of you to take such an interest in my cousin's welfare."

It was at that point that Jacob Carstairs, who'd seemed livid with rage, appeared to remember himself, and, dropping the furious gaze, looked a bit ashamed . . . as well he ought, thought Victoria with some satisfaction.

"Your concern for my future is much appreciated," she said, a little let down that this, then, were all the fireworks to which they were to be treated. "But I can assure you, you have nothing to fear. I am quite capable of making my own decisions, Captain. I have been doing so all my life, you know."

Captain Carstairs only shook his head. "There are dangers here in England you've never dreamed of, my lady. And I'm not talking about scorpions or quicksand. Or," he added even more ominously, "tureen of beef two nights in a row."

This sounded thrillingly portentous . . . enough so that Victoria's pulse quickened, and she leaned toward Jacob Carstairs eagerly.

"What do you mean?" she asked breathlessly. "Captain Carstairs, do you know something about my fiancé that I don't?"

But Jacob crushed her hopes of finding out that Lord Malfrey had a hidden deformity or a mad twin brother with whom he occasionally traded places by saying curtly, "Only that he is not a man of honor."

This was such a disappointing response that Victoria rolled her eyes. "Is that all?" she asked.

"Isn't that enough?" Captain Carstairs demanded, his dark brows furrowed.

Rebecca, who'd been standing nearby the whole time, piped up with, "It is a very serious accusation, Vicky. I am certain it is not one the captain would make lightly."

"I'm sure you are right," Victoria said, so as not to hurt

her cousin's feelings. She was not, however, the least impressed by the captain's warning. Why, her uncles had often accused men under their command of being less than honorable. But these charges almost always turned out to stem from the dullest of crimes, such as not keeping their mistresses in very high style, or failing to see their horses properly watered after a long ride. Victoria supposed the captain had some equally boring charge to lay at the feet of the earl, and in truth, she could not have been less interested in hearing it.

"La," she said when she felt enough time had passed that Rebecca and Captain Carstairs would think her suitably chastened. "Shall we go pitch biscuits out the window at the dogs?" For this seemed to Victoria the most entertaining activity that Almack's had to offer thus far. She'd noticed some of the younger boys engaged in it, and quite envied them.

Rebecca and Jacob Carstairs exchanged meaningful glances.

"Vicky," Rebecca said, "I don't think you quite understand what the captain is trying to tell you."

Victoria rolled her eyes again. Lord, what was wrong with the English? They did go on and on about things—but not the right kinds of things. Really, if it hadn't been for Victoria, the Gardiners might have had tureen of beef seven nights a week and not uttered a peep about it. But about something as trivial as whom she was to marry, no one seemed capable of remaining silent.

It was all Captain Carstairs's fault, of course. *Odious man!* Victoria was going to have to find someone new for Becky to love, and posthaste. She noticed a promising-looking fair-haired young man standing a little ways away, saw with approval that his mustache was neatly trimmed and his collar points high, and tossed her fan surreptitiously in his direction, then exclaimed, looking down at her bare wrist in horror, "My fan! Oh, Becky! I've lost my fan!"

Rebecca, always highly sensitive to calamities such as these, immediately lifted her hem and glanced about the floor.

"You had it a moment ago," she said reassuringly. "I'm almost certain."

"Oh, if it's trodden upon," Victoria wailed, "I shall be sick! Positively sick!"

She was aware that Captain Carstairs was watching her with a very skeptical expression on his face, one dark eyebrow lifted with the other furrowed disapprovingly. But she steadfastly ignored him, keeping her gaze on the floor as she "searched" for her fan.

"Is this what you're looking for, my lady?" asked the fair-haired gentleman with a smile as he held out Victoria's fan, which he'd bent and retrieved from where it had fallen at his feet.

"Oh, there it is!" Rebecca cried gladly. "And look,

Vicky, it isn't a bit trodden on."

Victoria accepted her fan with a grateful glance in the blond gentleman's direction. "You are too kind, sir," she said. "It is good to know that there are *some* gentlemen left in England." She shot a dark look in Jacob Carstairs's direction. "Might I know the name of my chivalrous rescuer?"

The blond gentleman blushed charmingly.

"Abbott, my lady," he said. "Charles Abbott."

"How lovely to make your acquaintance, Mr. Abbott," Victoria said, relieved that Charles Abbott proved to have neither a lisp nor a stutter. He would, she decided, do very nicely for Rebecca, as Victoria, who had a quick eye, observed that Mr. Charles Abbott wore a signet ring, but no wedding band, upon his finger, meaning that he was in possession of some fortune, but not a wife. "I, of course, am Lady Victoria Arbuthnot, and this is my cousin, Miss Rebecca Gardiner." Rebecca curtsied prettily in response to Charles Abbott's bow. "Oh," Victoria added with deliberate indifference, "and this is Captain Jacob Carstairs."

Charles Abbott clicked his heels together smartly upon his introduction to Jacob Carstairs, but his gaze was, Victoria saw with approval, on Rebecca, who really did look very beautiful indeed in her borrowed finery.

"She likes opera and the works of Sir Walter Scott," Victoria whispered to Mr. Abbott, under pretense of flicking a piece of lint from the young man's broad shoulder.

Charles Abbott proved he was as quick as he was

handsome, since the next words out of his mouth were, "You would not happen to be familiar with *The Lay of the Minstrel*, would you, Miss Gardiner? For there is a point in it these fellows here and I find sorely perplexing . . . ."

Victoria saw that her cousin looked very pleased indeed, but did not hear how she responded, since Jacob Carstairs leaned down and said, very distinctly, in her ear, "Witch."

Victoria had no choice but to take umbrage at this unfair assessment of her character.

"I beg your pardon, sir," she said with a sniff. "But I don't know what you mean."

"You manage your relations the way Napoleon manages his troops," Jacob Carstairs said, not entirely without approval.

Victoria flicked opened her fan. "Nonsense," she said, fanning herself energetically, though still keeping a careful eye on her cousin and her new admirer.

"Are the Gardiners even aware," Jacob wanted to know, "of how you've twisted their lives about to suit your own? I understand their cook is terrified to serve anything but lobster turbot—which, if I recall rightly, was your favorite dish back on the *Harmony*—and that the younger Gardiners have actually begun acting like little ladies and gentlemen because you promised if they'd behave themselves to buy them a live monkey."

"I can't even begin to imagine what you're talking about," Victoria said airily.

"I suppose that's your plan with Hugo Rothschild," Jacob said. "You intend to turn him into an automaton, the way you have the Gardiner children."

"Automaton?" Victoria echoed with a snort. "Be your age, Captain. What on earth would Lord Malfrey do with a monkey? What nonsense."

"It isn't nonsense," Jacob said. Something about his gaze, as he stared down at her, began to make Victoria feel distinctly uncomfortable. Jacob Carstairs's gray eyes were entirely too knowing—and too bright—for Victoria's peace of mind. Why, the way he looked at her, she felt almost as if . . . well, as if he could read her mind! Read her mind, or see down her bodice, she didn't know which. Either way, his stare was making her feel as if the room were too hot—it was—and her corset stays too tight—they weren't. How curious that a man she despised as thoroughly as Victoria despised Captain Carstairs could make her feel so . . . well, vulnerable.

A second later she was certain he *could* read her mind when he warned, "One day, Lady Victoria, you're going to meet a man whose will can't be bent to suit your purposes. And I'm not talking about Lord Malfrey, either. I mean a real man. And when that happens . . ."

Victoria raised her eyebrows. "Yes?" she inquired.

"You'll fall in love with him," Jacob Carstairs said shortly.

Victoria could not help laughing very heartily at that.

"Oh, Captain!" she cried, flinging out a hand to keep him from saying more—for surely if he did, she'd die laughing. "You are so droll! As if I could ever love anyone but Hugo!"

But Jacob Carstairs wasn't laughing at all. He regarded her gravely with those sea-gray eyes, looking almost—she did not think she was imagining this—as if he felt sorry for her.

Sorry! For *her*! Lady Victoria Arbuthnot, who had forty thousand pounds! Really, it was *too* excessively diverting.

"You don't love him," Jacob said somberly. "You can't possibly."

It was then that, out of the corner of her eye, Victoria caught a glimpse of something. She could not say what it was, exactly, that caused her to turn her head just when she did. All she knew was that, in spite of how very, very interesting she found what Jacob Carstairs was saying, she could not seem to keep her gaze upon his face. Instead she glanced over her shoulder, back toward the doors to the room they were standing in. . . .

And found herself looking at the handsomest man she had ever seen. A man in evening dress, with golden hair, a manly jaw, and a smile just for Victoria.

"Oh, can't I, then?" she asked Jacob with a radiant smile.

And then she turned to fly into her fiancé's waiting arms.

CHAPTER SIX

"Well?" Victoria spun in a circle before Lord Malfrey. "How do I look?"

"Pretty as a picture," his lordship declared. "Prettier, even."

Victoria stopped spinning, then ran her hands nervously over her muslin skirt to smooth it. Her fiancé's assertion was all well and good, but she felt she might need a less subjective opinion. "Becky?" she asked, with a nervous glance in her cousin's direction.

But Rebecca was hardly paying attention. She had one hand up, shading her eyes—though the sun was putting in a halfhearted appearance, being mostly hidden behind the clouds that seemed perpetually to cover the English sky—while she scanned the green lawn before them.

"I don't see him," she said, sounding dismayed. "Are you sure Mr. Abbott received an invitation, Lord Malfrey?"

"Of course I'm sure, Miss Gardiner," Hugo said with a laugh. "I added his name to the guest list myself. Now tell your cousin how lovely she looks, so we can join the rest of the company."

Rebecca threw Victoria a glance that could only be called perfunctory. "Vicky, stop fussing," she said. "You look fine."

But this casual remark was hardly enough to satisfy Victoria, who had spent the whole of the morning in front of her bedroom mirror, castigating Mariah for not getting her hair coiled to perfection and her gown wrinkle-free. Nothing looked right—not her upswept hair, not the high-waisted white gown, not the blue silk sash just below her bosom, not the sapphire bobs in her ears, shimmering like stars, nor even the deceptively simple—but murderously expensive—blue-and-white straw bonnet she wore atop her head.

And Victoria wanted everything to look right, because today was the day every girl dreamed of . . . while at the same time fearing it with every fiber of her being. For today was the day Victoria was to meet for the first time the woman who would be her mother-in-law.

"Mother will love you!" Hugo had exclaimed, when Victoria had expressed her reservations about this meeting to him. "Are you mad? How could anyone *help* but love you, Vicky?"

But Victoria did not share her husband-to-be's confidence in the matter. She knew that every home could have only one chatelaine, and she was determined that, in Hugo's home, that would be she. But supposing the dowager Lady

Malfrey was unwilling to allow her to take charge?

Well, the dowager Lady Malfrey would simply have to be gotten rid of.

Oh, not by killing her, of course. Victoria had a profound distaste for violence, and besides thought murder entirely too easy—unsporting, actually. It would be far more challenging simply to try to convince Hugo's mother of the benefits of living elsewhere . . . Bath, perhaps. Or Portofino. Portofino was said to be lovely. . . .

Oh, it would be so much nicer if it didn't come to that! It would be so much nicer if Hugo's mother turned out to be rather a dim sort of woman, only too happy to allow Victoria to take over the running of her household. Or, better still, if she happened to turn out to be a shrewd woman who recognized at once Victoria's superior management skills, and stepped dutifully out of the way.

Either way, Victoria was about to find out just what, in fact, her future held: for Hugo had placed her hand upon his arm, and was steering her toward the large party gathered beneath one of the largest oaks in Hyde Park, for a festive picnic in honor of his bride-to-be.

When Hugo had mentioned that his mother wished to hold a bridal picnic, Victoria had wondered—to herself, of course—if the woman was not perhaps unsound in the head. But now that she approached the series of white sheets spread out upon the grass, and saw the uniformed footmen, in their powdered wigs and coattails, standing about with silver trays of champagne glasses and bowls of fat ripe strawberries dipped in sugar, she saw that the word *picnic*, in England, meant something far different than it did back in India. In India picnics were hardly popular affairs, thanks to the heat, the constant threat of attack by tigers or bandits, and the throngs of impoverished beggars that gathered around the picnic blankets with their palms stretched out and their mouths opened hungrily. Victoria had never once attended a picnic where she did not end up giving away three quarters of her own food to the less fortunate, while her uncles had always insisted on embarking on such outings with an armed escort of no less than twenty men . . . an undertaking that made picnics in their area hardly a popular form of entertainment.

Picnics in England were obviously something else entirely, if the coolly elegant scene before Victoria was any indication. There wasn't a tiger in sight, let alone any armed militiamen. If there were beggars, they certainly ventured nowhere near. And as for bandits, the closest to them Victoria could detect was another group of well-dressed picnickers a few hundred feet away.

Hugo guided Victoria toward a pleasantly plump older woman who had laugh lines radiating from the corners of her bright blue eyes, and a lot of very dark—surely dyed—curls peeping out from beneath her bonnet brim.

"Mother," Hugo said to the woman with a bow, "may I present at last my bride-to-be, Lady Victoria Arbuthnot."

Victoria, her heart beating wildly—for all she could think was, *Supposing she doesn't like me?*—curtsied prettily and said, "So honored to make your acquaintance, ma'am."

The dowager Lady Malfrey, however, was not one to stand on ceremony, since she instantly reached out and seized Victoria by both shoulders and pulled her in for a long—and rather tight, to Victoria's way of thinking—embrace.

"At last, at last!" cried the dowager Lady Malfrey. Her voice was quite childlike in its tenor and pitch. "I have heard so much about you, Lady Victoria, I feel as if I know you already! But you are so much prettier than anyone said. Hugo, why did you not tell me she was so very, very lovely?"

Hugo stood looking down upon them with a twinkle in his blue eyes—eyes that, Victoria saw now, he'd inherited from his mother.

"I believe I did," he said with a chuckle. "Did I not tell you she was fair as the evening star?"

To be compared to the evening star was, of course, a compliment beyond all compliments, and Victoria, blushing with pleasure, thought she might actually die from joy . . . but first she rather hoped to extricate herself from her future mother-in-law's embrace, as that good woman still held on to her with a surprisingly strong grip.

"We shall be the best of friends," the dowager declared, her cheek very soft upon Victoria's. "The best of friends,

I can already tell. Welcome . . . welcome, my child, to the family."

While this greeting was very nice indeed, it instantly set Victoria on her guard, for she knew very well that mothers- and daughters-in-law could never be friends. Allies, perhaps, against the men in the family, who would inevitably muddle things with their imprudent purchases and dirty boots. But never, ever friends. Victoria had listened as each of her ayah's daughters wept after moving in to her husband's home, only to find that the mother-in-law who had insisted before their wedding that they were the best of friends had turned around and spoken badly of her to the servants and all of her other daughters-in-law at the earliest opportunity.

No, friends with the dowager Victoria knew she would never be. But rampaging Zulu warriors would not have dragged the truth of this from her lips.

"How nice," she said instead, still wishing the dowager would release her. "I never had a mother, as I'm sure you know. At least, not one that I remember well."

"I shall be a mother to you," the dowager said, giving Victoria yet another rib-crunching squeeze. "A mother *and* a friend!"

"That will be splendid," Victoria said . . . and was able to draw breath at last when the older woman suddenly released her.

"Oh, no, not now," the dowager Lady Malfrey said in

a sharp tone that was quite unlike the one she'd used with Victoria. "The petit fours come *after* the lamb cutlets!"

Victoria turned her head and saw that the good lady was addressing one of the footmen, who was carrying a silver platter loaded down with tiny chocolate-covered pastries ... pastries that Victoria already recognized, even after the mere two weeks she'd been in London, as being from one of the finest bakeries in town.

While she was, of course, honored that the dowager would go to so much expense on her account, Victoria could not help suspecting that, after her marriage, she was going to be presented with the bill for this little party. For there were, by her count, nearly fifty guests, who would each consume half a bottle of champagne at least (for despite the lack of sun, it was a warmish day). Then there was the cost of hiring the footmen, not to mention the food—lamb cutlets, as Victoria knew only too well from her now-daily consultations with the Gardiners' cook, were not cheap—and the rental of the silverware ...

Why, Victoria would not be surprised if the whole picnic ran over a hundred pounds! A hundred pounds! And spent by a woman who supposedly didn't have a penny to her name!

Oh, no. Victoria and her future mother-in-law were definitely *not* going to be friends. Not when Victoria began what she knew was going to be the very arduous task of forcing Hugo to retrench. For even her forty thousand pounds would not last, if this was a typical example of how the Rothschilds entertained.

"Isn't it a lovely party?" her cousin asked her dreamily an hour or so later. Victoria, who had had her fill of crab cakes and oysters—not to mention Lord Malfrey's friends, who were of the hearty, backslapping variety—had taken up her parasol and begun to stroll around the edges of the picnic area . . . allegedly to walk off the effects of the champagne, but actually so that she could keep an eye on the servants, whom she'd begun to suspect were palming the silver.

"Yes," Victoria replied without having really heard the question. There was something amiss about the dowager Lady Malfrey's friends . . . many of them, like the dowager, had dyed hair. And their clothes seemed . . . well, a bit *bright*. They had all been very charming to Victoria, but there was no escaping the fact that they seemed to her to be rather . . . common. None of the men seemed to have employment, and she'd fancied that several of the women were wearing face powder. And Victoria was ready to swear that one of the younger ones had actually arrived with her skirts damp—on purpose, to make the material cling to her admittedly well-shaped legs.

Her aunt Beatrice, Victoria knew, would have suffered apoplexy had she witnessed such a thing. Victoria was very glad that her aunt and uncle had had a prior social commitment and could not attend the hastily arranged picnic.

"And you know," Rebecca prattled on, swinging her reticule gaily beside her as she strolled, "Mr. Abbott says it's the loveliest picnic he's ever been to."

Victoria did not doubt this was so. It was also most likely the costliest.

But seeing that Rebecca was so happy lifted her spirits a bit. Victoria even went so far as to congratulate herself that it was all due entirely to her own careful planning. Charles Abbott had proved to be an attentive and ardent suitor. More important, however, he had turned out to possess a fortune of five thousand a year, which, while not as impressive as Jacob Carstairs's income, was nevertheless far more than a girl of Rebecca's comparatively modest means could reasonably expect in a suitor. It had not been at all difficult to convince Mr. Abbott—who, at one and twenty, was quite ready to fall in love—of her cousin's merits.

And it had been even easier to get Rebecca to forget all about her infatuation with a certain ship captain, and think only of Mr. Abbott instead. For as Victoria knew very well indeed, there was nothing more appealing to a young girl than a handsome gentleman who happens to admire her. All it took was a few well-timed compliments and a nosegay in order for Mr. Abbott to replace Captain Carstairs in Miss Gardiner's heart. Her hand, Victoria was certain, would soon be his.

"The dowager," Rebecca observed as they ambled

along the edge of one of the picnic sheets, "seems a very jolly sort."

"Doesn't she?" Victoria was thinking that the dowager had every reason to feel jolly . . . her financial concerns were soon to evaporate entirely.

"I only hope that Charles's mother will be as welcoming of me," Rebecca said with a nervous giggle—for as she and Mr. Abbott were not yet engaged, it was rather daring of her to call him by his first name. "When the occasion arises, I mean."

"I'm certain she will," Victoria said warmly. "For what mother would not welcome a daughter-in-law like you? You embroider so tidily, and I've never heard *you* raise your voice to the servants."

Rebecca looked pleased. "I hope you're right! But Mr. Abbott and I are not even engaged yet, so it's wrong of me even to think of such things. You, however . . . oh, Vicky, it's like a dream, isn't it? I mean, the way Lord Malfrey worships you."

Victoria had to admit that it was. For all her irritation with the Rothschilds' friends, and the way Hugo and his mother mismanaged their limited income—for the dowager was not alone in her profligate spending habits; her son, too, bore some of the blame—it was difficult to stay angry with either of them. Hugo was, of course, all that was romantic and tender, constantly reminding Victoria of how precious she was to him, and stealing kisses whenever

he was able. He'd even gone so far as to spend part of the
money he'd taken to Lisbon to retrieve his familial portraits on an engagement ring, which Victoria now wore
instead of his signet on her wedding finger. Never mind
that the emerald—which Hugo had insisted matched
Victoria's hazel eyes, a mistake for which she readily for-
gave him—was larger than Victoria thought strictly taste-
ful. It had been a lovely gesture. And as soon as they were
married, Victoria would have the stone recut to a more
modest size. And she'd have a pair of ear bobs to match!

Hugo had even managed to soothe the Gardiners' fears
concerning his impending wedding to their headstrong
niece. By becoming a familiar guest in the Gardiner household and getting to know each of the little Gardiners by
name, he had charmed Victoria's aunt. And with his frequent
gifts of cigars to Victoria's uncle, he had managed to win
that man's favor as well. Her aunt and uncle had given them
their blessing, and now that Hugo's mother seemed pleased
with the match as well, Victoria supposed the only thing left
to do was settle upon a date. She rather fancied getting married on a Tuesday. She had always been fond of Tuesdays.

Victoria was planning her honeymoon in Venice—she
had heard Venice was lovely—when, beside her, Rebecca
suddenly stiffened and sucked in her breath.

"I say," Rebecca exclaimed as they reached the edge
of the farthest picnic sheet. "Isn't that . . . Why, Vicky, I
think . . . Yes, it is; it *is* him! What is *he* doing here?"

Victoria looked in the direction Rebecca was pointing. There, coming toward them from the riding path, on a handsome bay with a nicely arched neck, was Captain Jacob Carstairs . . . whose name, Victoria knew for certain, was *not* on the dowager Lady Malfrey's guest list. Victoria was the one, in fact, who'd insisted on its not being there.

"Stuff and bother," Victoria muttered, lowering the brim of her parasol so it covered her face. It was probably a hopeless gesture, but there was always a chance the captain hadn't yet recognized her. Besides, the parasol hid the blush that unaccountably—and very annoyingly—showed up on Victoria's cheeks every time she encountered Jacob Carstairs of late.

Which was ridiculous, because of course she was in love—deeply and irrevocably in love—with the ninth Earl of Malfrey. Surely the only reason she happened to blush when Jacob Carstairs looked her way had to do with the fact that the captain was so very forward. He did, after all, seem to think he knew what was best for her—and had no compunction about telling her so.

Though she tried standing quite still—the way a rabbit, caught in the path of a cobra, often did—Jacob Carstairs seemed to notice her just the same, since soon a pair of horse's hooves appeared in the grass before her, and Victoria heard Captain Carstairs say, in that infuriatingly teasing tone of his, "Good afternoon, Lady Victoria, Miss Gardiner."

Victoria had no choice then but to raise her parasol

and smile sunnily into his insufferably smug face.

"Captain," she said, her calm tone at odds with the high color in her cheeks.

Beside her, Rebecca, whom she'd thought sufficiently recovered from her infatuation with the ship captain, was proving that this was not the case. She had turned as pink in the face as Victoria, and seemed not to know where to place her gaze. Victoria glanced frantically around for Mr. Abbott, but he was, the selfish thing, engaged in a game of mumblety-peg and not even looking in their direction.

"Not a very promising day for a picnic," Captain Carstairs said with a glance at the leaden sky above.

"At least it's warm," Victoria replied. Inside, of course, her response was not nearly so sanguine. *Weather? You stand there discussing the weather with him, with this obnoxious man who seems to think he knows what's best for you, and who has, probably for good, broken the heart of your most beloved cousin? What is wrong with you? Tell him to take his horse and go to—*

"Is that the dowager Lady Malfrey I see?" Captain Carstairs asked, squinting in Victoria's future mother-in-law's direction.

"Indeed," Victoria replied tonelessly.

"Well." The captain, from high atop his saddle, scanned the assorted guests seated upon the white sheets and the footmen who moved about them with their bowls of sugared strawberries and trays of champagne. She prayed that Jacob Carstairs was not farsighted enough to see the damp-skirted young lady from his perch. "How nice."

Nice? *Nice?* That was all he had to say? If that was all he had to say, why didn't he ride on? Why did he just sit there, looking out over the picnic blankets like a maharaja surveying his troops. . . ?

It was at this point that Rebecca suddenly let out a startled cry. "My reticule!"

Victoria turned her head and saw, of all things, a ragged little miscreant—male, apparently, though it was hard to tell beneath the dirt—dart by, clutching her cousin's bag.

Rebecca's shriek had startled the captain's horse—as, Victoria supposed, the thief knew it would; otherwise he would not have dared so bold a move, and in broad daylight . . . well, what passed for daylight in this damp place. Still, Jacob Carstairs handled the steed admirably, crying, "Stop, thief!" while still managing to keep his place in the saddle.

But the captain's aid—though appreciated—was not strictly needed. Not when Victoria had merely to stick out a foot and trip the recalcitrant young man, then rest her knee in the middle of his spine.

Nothing, of course, could have been simpler. But here came the earl and Mr. Abbott, along with the rest of the picnickers, as if there were something they could do, as well.

Really, Victoria thought with disgust, but Londoners made such a fuss about things!

CHAPTER SEVEN

"Oh, Lady Victoria!" the dowager Lady Malfrey cried. "Don't touch him! The dirty thing might . . . might *bite you* or something!"

Victoria regarded her future mother-in-law calmly from where she knelt, with one knee pressed firmly in the small of the little thief's back. The boy was kicking a great deal, and wailing quite lamentably as well, but wasn't otherwise causing Victoria the least bit of concern.

"Here you are, Becky," she said, plucking her cousin's reticule from the boy's hand, and passing it back to the older girl. "I'm sure he's very sorry for what he did. Aren't you?" She leaned more heavily on the boy's spine. "Aren't you?"

"Aye," the lad cried. "Aye! Let me up! Please let me up, miss!"

Captain Carstairs, who by this time had gotten his horse under control and dismounted, leaned down and laid rough hands upon the boy's shoulder.

"It's all right, my lady," he said to Victoria. "I've got him now."

Victoria, noticing how close Jacob Carstairs's face was to hers, and how, though he wasn't anywhere near as handsome as the earl—not with those collar points!—very amiable he looked, nonetheless rose quickly, so as to be as far from him as possible.

"Well, let's get a look at you, then," the captain said, hauling the boy to his feet.

The thief was not, Victoria soon saw, a very prepossessing creature. Although he was covered in dirt, from his scuffed boots to his mop of lank hair, there was a fist-sized clean spot in the center of his face—but this was only because the frightened boy was weeping.

"Please, sir," he begged between sobs. "Don't call the Runners on me, sir."

Runners, the dowager Lady Malfrey explained sotto voce to a perplexed Victoria, were the Bow Street Runners, who kept the peace in the streets of London.

"They'll hang me, sir." The boy sobbed. "They already hung me dad."

Victoria raised her eyebrows when she heard this. She was not opposed to punishing criminals, but hanging thieves seemed to her to be a bit extreme. In India such a crime would have earned so young a boy a mere whipping. Really, but the justice system in England seemed a bit harsh, sending tax evaders halfway across the world to live amongst the kangaroos, and hanging poor little purse snatchers! Victoria had had no idea things were so very strict here.

"Got him, then, Carstairs?" Lord Malfrey came striding up. "Little ruffian! Victoria, are you quite all right?"

"Of course I am," she said. Imagine, making such a fuss over a simple footpad! "Rebecca's the one whose purse was stolen, not me."

All eyes turned toward Rebecca, who was crying almost as fitfully as the boy—although from fear, not because she'd been physically harmed. Victoria was certain the thief hadn't so much as bumped her.

"Are you all right, Miss Gardiner?" Charles Abbott asked with a look of genuine—and tender—concern.

"Oh!" was all Rebecca seemed able to say. The next thing Victoria knew her cousin had thrown herself, weeping stormily, into Mr. Abbott's strong arms. He looked surprised but delighted by this turn of events, and was soon guiding Rebecca away from the scene, with one arm curled protectively around her slender shoulders. Seeing this, Victoria shot a triumphant look in Captain Carstairs's direction, eager to see how he would take the abandonment of a girl Victoria was certain he'd once numbered amongst his conquests.

To her disappointment, however, Jacob Carstairs wasn't paying the slightest bit of attention to Rebecca Gardiner. All of his powers of concentration seemed focused on the footpad he was now holding by the collar of the boy's shirt.

"Someone must go for the Runners at once," Lord

Malfrey was saying. "I'll hold the boy, Carstairs. Take your horse and go for the magistrates."

But Jacob Carstairs dismissed this with a curt, "You take my horse. I'll stay here and hold him."

"It's *your* horse," Hugo pointed out, not very nicely.

Jacob Carstairs grinned in a manner Victoria could only call wicked. "Afraid you won't be able to manage him, Malfrey?"

The earl looked affronted. "Certainly not! Only that . . . well, it's my fiancée who's been insulted. I'm the one who ought to stay and comfort her."

Everyone turned to look at Victoria, who, to her own certain knowledge, was far from needing any comfort. She was quick to admit as much, saying, "*I* haven't been insulted. And I certainly don't need comforting. I'm perfectly all right."

Seeing Lord Malfrey's slightly disappointed look—not to mention the way his mother shook her head until her black (surely a woman of that age should have *some* gray in her hair) curls swayed—Victoria bit her lip. Clearly she ought to have feigned light-headedness or something. Catching footpads with her bare hands, like descending ladders from boats, was obviously not something proper English ladies were supposed to do. *When* was she going to learn? She would never make a very good earl's wife at this rate.

"Please, sirs," the boy the captain held so tightly wailed.

"I swear I'll never do it again, if you'll only let me go!"

He sounded, to Victoria's ears, perfectly truthful. The boy looked terrified out of his mind.

The dowager Lady Malfrey apparently did not think so, however, since she said, "Stop standing about arguing with the man, Hugo, and go and fetch a Runner so we might all get back to our picnic!"

Hugo, glaring darkly, turned to seize the reins of Captain Carstairs's mount. It was at that point that Victoria decided she had had quite enough of the entire situation. Whether or not it was proper for young English ladies to go about catching footpads, she didn't know. But one thing she did know: it wasn't proper to hang little boys.

And so, accordingly, she thrust a finger at a point in the air just above the captain's right shoulder and let out a bloodcurdling shriek.

As Victoria had hoped, Jacob was so startled he loosened his hold on the boy momentarily. "What?" he cried, turning his head toward the direction in which she pointed. "What is it?"

The footpad, who was clearly no one's fool, took off at a pace so incredibly fast, it was doubtful even Captain Carstairs's horse would have been able to overtake him—providing the captain had mounted him in time. Which he did not, in fact, do. Instead Jacob Carstairs, realizing at once what Victoria had done—and why—turned to look at her with an expression that could only have been called cynical.

"What?" Lord Malfrey was still searching for whatever had caused Victoria to scream so loudly. "What is it, my love? Gypsies? Never say Gypsies have dared showed their faces in Hyde Park!" Then, noticing that the footpad had escaped, he cried, "Carstairs, you great ass! You let him get away!"

Jacob Carstairs turned his cynical expression toward the earl. "So did you," he observed.

"Are you mad?" Lord Malfrey wanted to know. "He'll only steal some other poor young lady's bag."

"Tell that," Jacob said dryly, "to your fiancée."

Lord Malfrey swung toward Victoria with a stunned expression on his handsome face. "Vicky," he cried. "Did you . . . did you scream apurpose? So the boy could get away?"

Victoria looked heavenward. "Oh, dear," she said, her gaze on the clouds. "Do you think it's going to rain? It doesn't look very promising, does it, my lord?"

"Victoria!" Lord Malfrey was shocked. "You can't allow scamps like that to run free! Why, he might murder the next person he robs!"

"He looked eager to reform his ways to me, my lord," Victoria said mildly.

"What can you even know of it?" Lord Malfrey wanted to know. "You're far too innocent to be acquainted with people of his sort—for which all I can say is, thank God. But I assure you, my lady, rogues like that can never be reformed!"

Victoria could not help darting a glance in Jacob Carstairs's direction upon hearing the word *rogue* from her fiancé's lips. She looked just in time to see the captain smother a laugh. *Insufferable young man!* By rights he really ought to have been horsewhipped by someone.

"I think you're wrong, my lord," Victoria said evenly, speaking to Hugo though her gaze was on Captain Carstairs. "I believe *no* rogue is beyond reforming."

Captain Carstairs, to Victoria's surprise, abruptly stopped laughing. His expression was very serious indeed as he swung back into his mount's saddle.

Victoria could not resist inquiring acidly, "Going so soon, Captain?"

"I'm late to an appointment as it is," Jacob Carstairs replied from his seat so high above her, with a smile completely devoid of warmth. "And I wouldn't want to keep you any longer from your little party."

"Kind of you, Carstairs," Lord Malfrey said, taking Victoria's hand and pressing it against the crook of his arm . . .

. . . an action Jacob Carstairs observed with a distinct tightening of his lips before curtly saying, "If I see a Runner, I'll give him the boy's description. We aren't complete barbarians here in England, Lady Victoria, whatever you might think. The child would not have been hanged. He only said that to play upon your heartstrings. It worked quite handily, I see. Well." He lifted his hat briefly. "Good day." Then he rode off.

He was, Victoria could not help noticing, an excellent horseman, who kept a very nice seat on his fractious steed. She oughtn't to have been surprised, she supposed, that Jacob Carstairs was as graceful on a horse as he was upon a ship. The wretched man seemed at ease wherever he happened to turn up.

Something that Lord Malfrey evidently noticed as well, if his next words were any indication.

"I say," Lord Malfrey declared. "That fellow does tend to appear at your side with alarming regularity, Victoria. I believe he might be a little in love with you."

Victoria, flicking a wary glance in Rebecca's direction—she was not fully convinced her cousin was completely over the dashing young captain—said, in a tone she hoped sounded quite unconcerned, "La, my lord, you could not be more mistaken! Jacob Carstairs has made it very clear indeed that I am his least favorite person in England."

"Well, he's a liar, then," the dowager Lady Malfrey declared from where she'd stood, along with everyone else, watching the excitement . . . for it wasn't every day a mother got to watch her son catch a footpad, even if, sadly, the heinous criminal had gotten away. "Because no one who met Lady Victoria could help but count her as one of their favorite people."

Victoria smiled, though her future mother-in-law's words made her feel distinctly uncomfortable. The dowager had not known her long enough, really, to make a judgment of this kind. She was, Victoria supposed, only being kind.

As, she was certain, her cousin was being as well, when she insisted to Victoria that she was not—no, not in the least!—upset over Lord Malfrey's remark about Jacob Carstairs being in love with Victoria.

"Lord Malfrey is in love with you himself, Vicky," Rebecca reminded her very nicely, as the two girls walked together back toward the picnic blankets. "Naturally he thinks everyone else should be, as well. Besides, I told you, I don't care a whit for Jacob Carstairs anymore. Mr. Abbott is ten times the man the captain is."

Victoria heard this with great approval. She agreed wholeheartedly, of course, and said so. Charles Abbott, she pointed out, was handsomer, kinder, and far, far more intelligent than Jacob Carstairs, because Charles Abbott had had the good taste to fall in love with Rebecca—not even to mention the fact that he wore his collar points at an appropriate height.

"I do think, however," Rebecca said, with a glance over her shoulder at their two suitors, who followed some few yards behind them, "that it wasn't entirely . . . well, lady-like of you to stop that boy the way you did. You really ought to have left it to the men."

Victoria heard this with raised eyebrows and a startled exclamation. "But, Becky, if I'd done that, he'd have gotten away with your bag!"

"So I'd have lost a hair comb and fifty pence," Rebecca said with a shrug. "It would not have been as bad as losing my dignity, which I fear you did a bit, Vicky, when you . . . well, did what you did. Why, even now, some of your hair's hanging down."

Victoria reached up to tuck the wayward strand back beneath her bonnet. She felt a prickle of irritation with her cousin, whom she could only decide was the most ungrateful creature on earth. After all she'd done for her, too, first convincing her of Jacob Carstairs's lack of worth as a potential husband, then arranging for the very handsome and desirable Mr. Abbott to fall in love with her, and then rescuing her reticule! Why, this was not even including the incredible improvements Victoria had made on her cousin's home, what with the banishment of the tureen of beef, the turning of Mariah into an undeniably professional lady's maid, and forcing her younger cousins to act like quiet, well-behaved boys and girls.

And this was the thanks she got for all her very hard work! 'Not entirely ladylike!'

It seemed to Victoria as if her many talents might never be suitably recognized—or appreciated—by anyone. For in order to complete the transformation she was planning on Lord Malfrey—turning him from titled but penniless peer into a man of wealth as well as privilege—she would have to progress with careful subtlety, so that he might never know she was managing him all along. For men hated nothing more than a woman who meddled in their business. Weren't her uncles a prime example? Why, they had sent her all the way to England when it finally dawned upon them that that was precisely what she'd been doing since the age of five.

Well, it was, she supposed, the cross that people such as herself must bear. It was entirely possible that her most selfless actions might never be acknowledged by those for whom they were exerted. Sad, but true.

Still, Victoria would not allow self-pity to creep into her thoughts. She had a good deal to be thankful for, after all, and those things included, of course, her forty thousand pounds, her sound teeth and constitution, her exceptionally fine ankles, and most important, her talent for tidying up things that had become, well, messy. For who didn't long for an existence free from unpleasant drama and catastrophes? That was why people like Victoria had been put upon the earth: to work at preventing such things.

And as soon as she was married, Victoria knew the very first catastrophe she'd correct: her mother-in-law's hair. If the dowager could not be persuaded to allow it to gray naturally, Victoria could, at least, convince her to wear a wig in a more natural shade than the ebony black of her current tresses.

Really, but it did seem at times as if Victoria's work might never be done. She still had all of the footmen's coat sleeves to search, as well. Because over her dead body was a single one of them going to escape with a scrap of the silver her future mother-in-law had hired for the occasion.

At Victoria's expense, of course.

CHAPTER EIGHT

"But are you certain you *want* to go, Becky?" Victoria inquired of her cousin, with what she hoped would be taken for very ladylike concern. "Because we needn't stay if you don't feel entirely up to it."

Rebecca, descending from the coach-and-four with care, for she was attired in another of Victoria's borrowed gowns, this one in the palest of pinks, looked cross.

"I told you before, Vicky," she said irritably, "it is nothing to me. *He* is nothing to me."

Victoria was very relieved to hear this. Still, she was not entirely convinced.

"Because we can still give our excuses, you know," she said in a low voice as the two girls trailed behind Mr. and Mrs. Gardiner, as they ascended the stone steps to the front door of Jacob Carstairs's Mayfair town house. "We can say I'm not feeling well, and turn right around for home."

Becky cast her cousin a disparaging look over one slim shoulder. She had been, ever since learning of her mother's acceptance of Captain Carstairs's invitation to dine, coolly indifferent about the situation. But that, Victoria was quite certain, was all an act.

Or so Victoria had thought, until her cousin's next words hit her like a slap in the face.

"If you ask me, Vicky," Rebecca said in a very sour voice, "*you're* the one who seems to have a problem dining at Captain Carstairs's table this evening. For *I* certainly don't care. My affections belong entirely to another now."

Victoria, exceedingly taken aback, declared, "I beg your pardon, Becky, but I do *not* have a problem with dining at Captain Carstairs's table this evening. Far from it. It's *you* I cannot help feeling concerned for. You did, after all, once confess yourself in love with him."

"I'm not half as in love with him as you are, Vicky," said Becky very snidely indeed.

And when Victoria—as she had every right to—let out a snort of indignation at this, her cousin had the nerve to add, "Well, anyone who hates a man half so much as you profess to hate Captain Carstairs can only be in love with him. In fact, I think Lord Malfrey and I got it all wrong: It isn't the captain who's in love with you. It's you who's in love with the captain."

It was on the tip of Victoria's tongue to tell her cousin precisely what she thought of this very absurd statement—not to mention what she thought of Becky herself—when the front door to Captain Carstairs's town house was thrown open, and they were all ushered inside by an extremely competent butler.

"Girls," Victoria's aunt said through gritted teeth as her wrap was being taken, "kindly do not squabble so. Mr. Gardiner and I would like to have a pleasant meal with Captain Carstairs and his mother."

"*I* am not the one who is squabbling," Victoria asserted, flattening a hand to her chest. "I am only defend-ing myself against your daughter, who seems to be casting aspersions against my character."

Becky said in a hiss, "I am doing nothing of the kind!"

"What do you call accusing a person of being engaged to one man but in love with another?" Victoria replied in a hiss of her own.

"I call her by her name, Lady Victoria Arbuthnot," Becky snapped.

And in truth it was a good thing that Captain Carstairs's butler announced them just then, or Cousin Becky might have found her ears boxed; Victoria was *that* incensed.

Well, and what else could she have expected, really? Victoria's ayah had warned her that few, if any, people seemed to know what was best for them, and that Victoria should not expect anyone to be grateful for the very kind help she was continuously offering them. The red ants Victoria saved from drowning by coaxing them onto a stick and rescuing them from the gardener's watering can would turn around and sting her at their first opportunity. And the mongrel she saved from the village children's stones would bite her, even as she attempted to feed it.

But for Becky to have accused her of being in love with Jacob Carstairs—Jacob Carstairs! Why, that was the cruelest blow Victoria had ever received. What could Victoria ever have done to put such a ridiculous idea in her cousin's head? She had had nothing but contempt and ill words for Jacob Carstairs since the very unfortunate day they'd met. What could her cousin possibly be thinking?

The butler showed them into a well-appointed room, high ceilinged and very airy. Jacob Carstairs's home, Victoria saw at once, was pleasant and tastefully decorated. This was due entirely, Victoria was certain, to the handsome and dignified woman introduced to her as Mrs. Carstairs, Jacob's mother, who clasped her hand warmly and said, "Lady Victoria, what a pleasure to meet you."

Mrs. Carstairs, Victoria noted with approval, had allowed her hair to turn gray, and the silver tinge added considerably to the lady's charm. It was, in fact, incredible to Victoria that so unaffected and natural a woman could have given birth to an unpleasant young man like Jacob Carstairs.

That individual stood by the fire—lit, of course, for though it was summer it rained, as it had virtually without stopping since Victoria's arrival—looking very content with himself indeed. Well, and why shouldn't he? Clearly his intention in inviting Victoria to dine in his home was to show her how very wrong she'd been in her low estimation of him. Wasn't that a Gainsborough hanging above his mantel? And weren't those Dresden shepherdesses on his sideboard? As if, simply because he owned these fine things, his opinion on Lord Malfrey's character ought to be trusted! *How rich.* Victoria wanted to laugh, but she was still too upset over her cousin's cruel remarks to do more than answer yes and no to Mrs. Carstairs's gentle questions about how Victoria was liking her stay in London thus far.

What, Victoria could only sit and wonder, as the others sipped champagne and chatted amiably about the very topics Victoria most adored, India and the military, could Becky have meant when she'd accused her of being in love with Captain Carstairs? Wasn't it perfectly obvious whom she was in love with? Wasn't she, in fact, wearing his ring?

Becky was merely jealous. Yes, that had to be it. Becky was still in love with Captain Carstairs, and she was jealous because Victoria was marrying the man of her dreams, while the man of Becky's dreams did not seem even to know she was alive. Really, if she thought about it, it was a very pitiable situation indeed. Poor Becky, still so deeply in love with the captain that she lashed out at the very person who'd tried so valiantly to cure her of that unfortunate malady! And poor Mr. Abbott, who was so genuinely smitten with the eldest Miss Gardiner!

But most of all, of course, poor Victoria, who was the one forced to bear the brunt of her cousin's unhappiness in the form of some very unfair barbs at her own expense!

Well, Victoria supposed there were martyrs who'd fared far worse and survived. Really, being accused of being in love with a man she could not abide was far better than being shot with poisoned darts or bitten by asps.

Or so Victoria supposed.

By the time the gong sounded for dinner, Victoria had roused herself with thoughts like these, and was actually able to join in on the conversation—which was, she had to admit, a far livelier one than any she'd enjoyed so far with her fiancé and his mother, who had a rather dull tendency to talk of nothing but people with whom Victoria was not acquainted. And the food, Victoria noted with approval, was superbly prepared and elegantly served, proving that Jacob Carstairs's mother was not only a charming hostess but competent with the staff as well, a pair of skills that rarely went hand in hand.

Really, Victoria thought with some amusement as she swallowed a mouthful of savory fruit compote. *It is just as well I am not in love with Jacob Carstairs—nor he with me—because it wouldn't do to marry him at all. His house is already perfect, run to perfection by his mother. And he already has money. Why, he doesn't need me a bit. I wouldn't have a thing to occupy my time all day long. I feel sorry for whomever he does end up marrying. She'll have a very dull time of it.*

Victoria became even more convinced of this when it came time for the men to disappear for cigars and brandy while the women repaired to the drawing room for coffee.

Mrs. Carstairs even gossiped divinely! She did not, of course, say anything that could at all be construed as malicious—she was much too ladylike for that—but she did mention a certain young lady whom her son had happened to see at a picnic at a park who—and here Victoria feared very much she would hear about her own little escapade with a certain footpad, and glanced nervously at Rebecca lest she give away the identity of this young lady with her surprised reaction. . . .

But it turned out she needn't have feared, since the young lady Mrs. Carstairs was speaking of was the one who'd dampened her skirts to make them cling more provocatively to her legs. Victoria blushed nonetheless, knowing now that Jacob *had* noticed the scandalously clad girl at Lord Malfrey's picnic, and had relayed her description—though not, apparently, the fact that Victoria and her cousin had been at the event as well.

"It really does make me so very relieved," Mrs. Carstairs went on as she passed Victoria a plate of sugared wafers, "that my own daughter is married and grown, with a baby of her own. For I do not think I could raise a girl in this day and age—though you, Beatrice, seem to manage quite well. Still, I don't envy you. So many young women today seem so wild! Imagine, soaking your skirts with water on purpose! Why, you could catch your death."

Victoria, nibbling on one of the wafers, regarded Mrs. Carstairs with interest. So Jacob had an elder sister! A sister old enough to be married with a child. How intriguing. Victoria could not picture the very self-assured captain with a sister, particularly an elder one. She wondered if Jacob's sister had ever tortured him when he was younger the way she and Rebecca, when they were very bored, enjoyed torturing her younger brothers, by sprinkling them with rosewater through the stairwell and dressing their hair in bows while they slept.

Victoria did not have time to wonder about this for long, since soon the men joined them again, and the conversation shifted back to less scandalous topics. The fact that there was to be a full moon that night, and that an eyeglass Captain Carstairs had ordered all the way from Italy was newly arrived, led everyone—with the exception of Mr. Gardiner, who had fallen asleep in a chair by the fire—out to the terrace leading off the drawing room, where they took turns peering through the lens—though with all the clouds, only the barest glimpse of the moon could be seen. The damp soon drove the other ladies back inside, but Victoria was determined to stay outside until she saw, as Rebecca had, the Dead Sea, and she refused to budge until the swiftly moving clouds overhead parted enough to award her a view.

To her irritation, Jacob Carstairs stayed outside as well . . . no doubt, she told herself bitterly, to make sure she did not drop or otherwise harm his precious new plaything.

"You needn't fear for footpads out *here*," she informed him very sarcastically. "I promise I shan't let anyone steal it."

"No," Captain Carstairs said with the tiniest of smiles, visible in the candlelight that spilled through the terrace doors. "I don't imagine that you would. I rather fear for any footpads that come your way."

Victoria snorted. "That certainly wasn't what you were saying the other day."

"I was in a foul mood the other day," Jacob admitted. "I meant to ask your pardon for that."

Victoria, exceedingly surprised that Jacob Carstairs would ask her pardon for anything, only raised her eyebrows, keeping her gaze on the bright patch in the clouds, behind which she knew loomed the moon.

"Aren't you going to ask me," Jacob asked, after some seconds of silence passed between them, "why I was in such a foul mood?"

"No," Victoria replied sweetly.

"Well, I intend to tell you anyway," Jacob said.

And then he did something so extraordinary that Victoria very nearly had to pinch herself to make certain she wasn't dreaming. He reached for the terrace doors, which had been left partly open, and pulled them shut. Then, from his waistcoat pocket, he extracted a key, and locked them . . .

. . . with the two of them outside!

Victoria—her eyes, she was quite sure, as large as

peacock eggs—inquired pointedly, "Are you mad?"

"Probably," Jacob Carstairs replied, dropping the key back into his pocket—which, Victoria supposed, was proof that he hadn't completely lost his mind . . . if he had, undoubtedly he'd have tossed the key over the side of the balcony. Then, reaching for one of the wrought iron chairs, he spun it toward Victoria, gave the damp seat a wipe with his handkerchief, and said, "Sit."

Victoria, very much affronted—but positively intrigued—by his behavior, replied with spirit, "I most certainly shall *not*."

"Fine," Jacob replied, putting the chair back where he'd gotten it. "Now you are going to listen to me."

Victoria realized that she did not have much of a choice. Unless she hurled herself over the side of the terrace—a drop of some twenty feet to the garden below—she could not help but listen to him. She supposed she could have banged on the terrace doors and alerted those inside of her plight. Her uncle Walter might be strong enough to break down the doors and rescue her . . . if he could be roused from his nap.

She was, however, mightily interested in what it was that Jacob Carstairs had gone to such drastic lengths to tell her. Were Hugo and Becky, she wondered, correct in their assertions that Captain Carstairs was in love with her? Was such a thing even possible? How could Jacob Carstairs possibly be in love with her, when for the entire time she'd known him he'd done nothing but vex and tease her? What sort of man showed his love for a woman in such a manner?

But then, recalling what Rebecca had said to her just that evening, it occurred to her that perhaps it was *because* of Jacob Carstairs's great passion for her that he'd taken to calling her Miss Bee and putting down her attempts to make things tidy. Perhaps what Rebecca had accused Victoria of—of hating Jacob Carstairs so passionately, she could only be in love with him—was actually true of the captain?

Good Lord! Could it be? It certainly seemed so! Was Jacob Carstairs going to confess his undying devotion to her, right here on his terrace, under the moonlight—well, what little there was of it—with his mother and her uncle and aunt just inside? Was he going to sweep her into his strong arms and rain impassioned kisses down upon her upturned face?

Victoria, much to her chagrin, found that the thought of Jacob Carstairs doing any of these things—confessing his love for her, sweeping her into his arms, and raining kisses down upon her face—was rather thrilling. In fact, just the thought that he might do any one of these things sent her heart beating a good deal more quickly than she knew it ought, considering the fact that she was engaged to someone else. What kind of girl was she, anyway, that she could find the idea of Jacob Carstairs kissing her so appealing? She was practically married! And to someone else!

And yet there was no denying that when the captain looked at her with those rain-cloud gray eyes and said her name, her pulse fluttered. And when he'd commanded her to sit, she'd felt quite a little jolt up and down her spine. There was nothing like a handsome man bossing one about . . . even if one hadn't the slightest intention of doing what he said.

La! she thought now. *He's going to admit, finally, that the reason he has this absurd prejudice against Lord Malfrey—and has been so nasty to me all these weeks—is because he is madly and passionately in love with me, and can't stand the thought of me in another man's arms! How very, very jolly! I shall be gentle with him, of course. I wouldn't want him to fling himself over the side of the balcony from a broken heart, or anything like that. He could crack his skull open on those garden boxes down there, and that would be so untidy. I shan't utter a peep about the collar points, either.*

"Victoria," Jacob said, and Victoria could not help thinking again that it was very presumptuous of him to call her by her given name when she had not given him permission to do so. But she supposed he was too maddened by love for her to be completely sensible of what he was doing.

"I've tried everything I can think of to convince you how foolhardy this scheme of yours is—of marrying Hugo Rothschild, I mean. But your aunt and uncle cannot—or will not—attempt to control you, and you will not seem to hear reason. And so you leave me with no choice but to reveal something to you—something that I

swore to myself I would never tell another living soul—
that I am afraid will only cause you pain . . . and myself
grievous injury as well."

Victoria thought this a very noble and dignified
speech. She knew, of course, what was to follow. He would
reveal his unrequited passion for her, and she, of course,
would act surprised, as if the idea of his being in love with
her had never, ever occurred to her. Then she would
politely tell him she did not return his affections, and
hoped he would not do anything rash.

"But the truth is, Victoria . . ." Here Jacob bent his dark
head, and seemed unable to go on.

Victoria, rather vexed that he wasn't coming right out
with it—surely her aunt would notice, sooner rather than
later, how long she'd been alone with him out on the terrace, and wonder what they were doing, and try the
door—decided to hurry things up a little. She laid a gentle hand upon his arm and said in the most comforting
voice she could summon, "Captain Carstairs, you needn't
say another word. You see, I already know."

Jacob looked up, and at that very moment the clouds
slid from the moon, sending an arc of bluish light onto the
balcony, and bringing into high relief the pain and sad res-
ignation etched upon his face.

"You do?" he asked in an astonished voice. "But how
did you . . . how could you have found out?"

"It doesn't matter," Victoria said gravely. "All that

matters is . . . well, what we're going to do about it."

"Do about it?" Jacob reached up to run a hand through his thick dark hair, causing Victoria's fingers to slip from his arm. But he seemed hardly to notice this. "What in God's name are you talking about? Isn't it obvious what you're going to have to do about it?"

Victoria saw that he was standing very close to the balcony railing. She would, she knew, have to handle this carefully indeed. While the idea of Jacob Carstairs doing himself an injury due to his great love for her was, of course, delightful, it had to be admitted that, much as he annoyed her, she would miss him if he expired. No one else ever looked at her with eyes that seemed to see right into her heart—even if Captain Carstairs had never given any indication that he liked what he saw there.

Besides, Victoria was certain Jacob's death would hurt his mother a good deal, and Mrs. Carstairs was a very nice woman whom Victoria would not have liked to see unhappy.

"Really, Jacob," she said, unconsciously using his given name for the first time in their acquaintance. "I think you're making far too much of this. I'm sure it's only . . . only a passing fancy."

"A passing fancy?" Jacob stared at her as if she'd just grown a second head. "That Hugo Rothschild is marrying you for your money? I rather think not."

CHAPTER NINE

Victoria, a good deal taken aback by this statement, blinked several times before managing to stammer, "Wh— what?"

Jacob stared down at her, his eyes in pools of shadow, as the moon had slipped behind the clouds once again.

"That *is* what you meant?" he asked. "When you said you already knew. Isn't it?"

"I . . ." Victoria was glad that the moon was gone. This way, though she could not read his expression, he, at least, could not see her blush.

Because Victoria was blushing, and deeply. Oh, what a fool she'd been, to think he was in love with her! Of course he meant only to harp on at her about the same old subject. Jacob Carstairs, in love with her? Perish the thought!

But it had to be admitted that Victoria felt more than a little disappointed that it was not so . . . which of course made no sense whatsoever, since she was in love with Hugo. What did *she* care how Jacob Carstairs felt about her?

"Of course that's what I thought you meant," Victoria said with a haughty toss of her head. "What else *could* you have meant?"

It was Jacob's turn to blink.

"I don't know," he said. "But you certainly seem cool enough about it."

"Well, it isn't exactly anything very new," Victoria said, pleased that he'd noted none of her discomfort. "You've been saying much the same thing—or something similar, anyway—since the moment I said yes to the earl's proposal."

"Yes, well"—he looked as serious as Victoria had ever seen him look—"now I intend to tell you the truth about your precious earl—the truth that I and only a few other people know. And I would ask that, because of the nature of what I'm about to reveal, you swear that you will never mention it to anyone, ever."

"It isn't ladylike to swear," Victoria reminded him primly.

"It isn't ladylike to tackle street urchins, either," Jacob pointed out. "But that didn't seem to stop you the other day."

Victoria lifted her gaze toward the heavens. "Very well," she said with a sigh. "I swear." And then, perhaps because she was a little disappointed that the captain wasn't, in fact, going to profess his undying devotion to her, she added with a good deal of asperity, "And now I suppose you're going to tell me a tawdry tale about some girl Lord Malfrey proposed to, then cast aside when he learned she hadn't as much money as he'd hoped."

"Pathetic is the word I'd use, not tawdry," Jacob said brusquely. "And it wasn't *some girl*. It was my sister."

Victoria brought her gaze very quickly to his face.

"Your . . . your sister?" she echoed. "But . . ."

And again she was grateful for the rain clouds, since they hid her suddenly flaming cheeks from sight. His *sister*? The one Mrs. Carstairs had spoken of, the one who was married and had a baby? Jacob Carstairs's sister and . . . *Hugo*?

He must have read the astonishment on her face, despite the absence of moonlight, since he said in a heavy voice, "Yes, my sister, Margaret. She married a Scot and lives in Edinburgh, or you'd have met her already. She's a great beauty, and was quite sought after when she came out a few years ago."

"I . . ." Victoria was so astonished she hardly knew what to say. All she could think was, *Stuff and bother!* Now there'd be nothing but endless trouble and tears for everyone involved.

But Jacob had paused, and she supposed he expected a response of some kind. So she murmured, "I didn't know."

"No," Jacob said, looking impatient. Evidently this was not the response he'd been anticipating. "How would you? You weren't even in England yet. In any case, Margaret could have had her pick of suitors, but the one she liked best was the man to whom you are now engaged—Hugo Rothschild. He wasn't Lord Malfrey then . . . his father was still alive, as was my own. The two of them were friends—

Malfrey's father and mine. Margaret and Rothschild were often thrown together as a result, and I suppose an engagement was inevitable. Three weeks before the wedding, however, disaster struck. Several of my father's ships were lost at sea due to a series of storms. His fortune seemed lost. The strain was too much for him and he fell ill, and never did completely recover. He died just six months later."

Victoria, who barely remembered her own father, said, "I'm so sorry," because it seemed the thing to say. But again Jacob brushed her response aside.

"It was while all this was happening—my father's illness, and the loss of his ships—that Hugo Rothschild told my sister he couldn't see his way toward marrying her after all. They would have nothing to live on, you see, since Hugo's father hadn't a penny to his name, either. Margaret suggested to Hugo that he might find work . . . an occupation. But Rothschilds, you see"—here the captain's voice took a derisive dip—"are above actually earning a living. They'd rather live, like parasites, off the earnings of others. And so Hugo left London, and my sister, never to be heard of again—until, that is, he showed up on the *Harmony*—which I found the height of cheek, that he should have returned to London on one of *my* ships. For upon my father's death, I took over the business, you see, and built it up again."

Victoria, who'd already heard this part of Jacob's story from Rebecca, could not help but admire Captain

Carstairs's narrative restraint. For he had not, as he'd so simply described, built his father's business up again, but rather started a new business, practically from scratch, which had gone on to flourish in a dramatically short period of time . . . the same amount of time that Lord Malfrey, if Jacob's story was to be believed, had been hiding in shame thousands of miles away.

It was, if it was true, a very serious charge indeed that Jacob Carstairs laid at the feet of Victoria's fiancé. For a broken engagement—and broken for such a reason!—was not soon to be forgiven. It was no small wonder that Hugo had not shown his face in England for so many years afterward.

But even though Victoria felt very sorry indeed for the former Miss Carstairs, who had doubtless had her heart broken and been slighted beyond imagining, she could not be insensible to the fact that the situation had not been an easy one for her fiancé, either. Was he to be blamed if, upon finding himself incapable of attaining it any other way, he attempted to marry money?

Still, if what Jacob was saying was true—and Victoria saw no reason why he might lie about it, when such a thing could so easily be checked—Lord Malfrey had behaved very badly indeed. For while Victoria had learned most of what she knew of romance from her ayah, from her uncles she had learned something even more important: sportsmanship. And a good sport accepted his losses gracefully, and took his lumps like a man. Running off to India and abandoning his bride might have been the most sensible thing for Lord Malfrey to have done—otherwise, without money or love (for it was clear from his behavior that the earl could not have loved Jacob's sister), what were the chances of the match succeeding? Still, it was hardly good sportsmanship. A game player took risks, and if those risks did not prove fruitful, then he took his lumps.

But Lord Malfrey had not taken his lumps. He had taken himself off instead. And that, to Victoria, was far more offensive than his attempt to marry for money.

But of course she couldn't admit as much out loud. She had, she could see now, made a terrible mistake in agreeing to marry Lord Malfrey. But it would be bad sportsmanship to admit as much to anyone else before she'd given the earl a chance to defend himself against the charges.

And she would *never* admit as much to the likes of Jacob Carstairs!

And so, masking her own feelings of wounded pride and, it must be admitted, some mortification—for what girl likes to hear that a man she thought was in love with her was marrying her only for money? Even a girl who'd suspected something of the kind all along, but had thought herself perfectly all right with the idea?—Victoria said gravely to Captain Carstairs, "I thank you for telling me. I am glad to hear that your sister's pain was not of long duration, and that she is happy now." Then, straightening herself up, Victoria gestured toward the terrace doors. "Now would you kindly unlock these? For I'd like to go inside again, if I may."

Captain Carstairs, who had, during his impassioned speech about his sister, come to stand very close to Victoria, now looked down at her with an expression every bit as astonished as if Victoria had suggested he walk barefoot across a bed of hot coals.

"Lady Victoria," he said in a voice that sounded a bit strangled. "I would never presume to tell you what to do—"

Victoria could not restrain an incredulous laugh at that. The captain ignored her.

"—however," he went on, "I would urge you to consider very carefully whether or not you ought to marry the earl. He isn't . . . well, he isn't a very good man. And though I know we have had our differences in the past, my lady"—and here the captain's gaze bored very hard into her own—"I do think that, for the most part, your extremely impertinent interference in the affairs of others stems from a genuine desire to do good."

Victoria parted her lips to protest that *interference* was hardly the correct term for her very kind efforts to improve the lots of her friends and relatives . . .

. . . but forgot everything she'd been about to say when she found one of her hands caught up in Captain

Carstairs's. Looking down at her slim fingers in his own much larger ones, Victoria felt, for some reason, her breath catch in her throat.

Which was, of course, perfectly ridiculous, because she didn't admire, much less care for, Captain Jacob Carstairs. Indeed, she considered him exactly what he'd just confessed to thinking her—a rude interferer. Only he, rather than interfering in the affairs of those less fortunate, seemed intent on constantly interfering in *hers*.

That fact, and that alone, was undoubtedly why, the moment Captain Carstairs's fingers closed over hers, Victoria's pulse seemed to grow erratic. And why her breath grew short. And her cheeks hotter than ever. Why, the impudence of the man! And the fact that that gray-eyed gaze seemed to be raking her face, taking in every little moonlit detail—for, of course, the moon *would* have come out again just then, when it was most inconvenient. Why, just who did Jacob Carstairs think he was?

"It would be a shame," the captain went on, keeping a firm grip on the hand that Victoria was attempting, albeit ineffectually, to slip from his grasp. He did not, however, seem to notice . . . or care, anyway. "A *burning* shame," he added forcefully, "were you to align yourself with a man who has never once considered doing anything for the good of anyone but himself."

Victoria found herself—beyond all reasoning, and much to her horror—being pulled hypnotically toward

Jacob Carstairs, as if his eyes were, of all things, the moon, and she the tide. It was completely illogical, but there it was, and there didn't seem to be a blessed thing she could do about it. Even as they stared at each other, their faces just inches apart, Victoria's body seemed to sway to fill the gap between them, in a manner of which she knew her ayah would have greatly disapproved.

But she couldn't seem to stop herself, though of course it defied all logic. She didn't even *like* Jacob Carstairs. Oh, certainly he was handsome enough, she supposed, in a darkly brooding sort of way. But those collar points! And that mouth—not to mention the things that seemed constantly to come out of it! How could she possibly feel attracted to such a person?

But what of *him*? For Jacob Carstairs had made it amply clear that she was not one of his favorite people. But he hadn't exactly dropped her hand and turned away in revulsion when she'd begun swaying toward him. Quite the opposite, as a matter of fact. *He* was swaying toward her as if as unable to stop himself as she was—

And then the worst thing possible occurred. Jacob Carstairs swayed so far forward that his mouth actually collided with hers.

The next thing Victoria knew, they were kissing. She and Jacob Carstairs, the last man on earth whose lips she'd *ever* want to touch with her own. Kissing! And quite passionately, too. Jacob had dropped her hand and reached out instead to seize her by both arms, as if fearful she'd sway so far forward the two of them would topple over the balcony railing, if he didn't attempt to stop her.

And she was no better! For her fingers had curled, as if of their own accord, around the back of the captain's neck, though Victoria could in no way determine how they'd gotten there, unless Jacob Carstairs had put them there . . . something she would not have put past him.

But, oh! It was strange how delightful it felt to have them there. Stranger still how delightful it felt to have Jacob Carstairs's mouth on hers! Which was, of course, perfectly ridiculous, because Victoria hated Jacob Carstairs—hated him with a passion, and, besides, was engaged to someone else . . . though, thanks to this evening's discoveries, she was not at all certain for how much longer.

Perhaps it was *because* she hated Jacob Carstairs so passionately that kissing him felt so terribly exciting. For love and hate were both very strong emotions, so naturally both would incite very strong reactions. She loved—or at least was very fond of—Lord Malfrey, and so being kissed by him was quite pleasurable. Why wouldn't being kissed by someone about whom she felt just as strongly—if not even more strongly—elicit a similar sensation?

Except, of course, that she doubted being kissed by someone one detested was supposed to trigger anything but feelings of revulsion. And she, oddly enough, felt far from revolted by Jacob Carstairs's kisses.

Oh, dear! For the first time since leaving India, Victoria found herself longing for her wise old ayah, who would surely have been able to clear up this very disturbing mystery for her—would have been able satisfactorily to explain why it was that, even though she hated Jacob Carstairs, the feel of his lips on hers made her heart beat so quickly inside her chest, she thought it might explode. Her heart had never beaten this quickly when Lord Malfrey kissed her . . . and he was her own fiancé! Something, Victoria felt sure, was very, very wrong. . . .

Especially considering the fact that, when Jacob lifted his lips from hers and started to say her name in a voice that sounded quite unlike his own, it was so ragged, Victoria only pulled his head down and started kissing him even more passionately than before. . . .

What might have happened if they'd remained undisturbed, Victoria later shuddered to think. He might possibly have proposed, and she might—*la! What a joke!*—possibly have accepted.

Fortunately, however, someone tried the terrace doors, and, hearing the latch rattle, the two of them sprang apart, Victoria with cheeks she was sure were scarlet, and Jacob with a dark curl of hair falling rakishly over one eye.

"Vicky?" Rebecca called, tugging on the latch. "Are you two still out there? Why won't the doors open? Are they stuck?"

Jacob, with a composure of mind Victoria quite envied, reached into his waistcoat pocket and withdrew the key.

"Yes," he said, in a voice that was a good deal steadier than any Victoria could have summoned. "They stick sometimes when it rains." Then, with one last penetrating—and, to Victoria, anyway, inscrutable—glance in her direction, he turned the key and opened the doors.

"Ah," he said, grinning in the rectangle of light that spilled out from the drawing room, and looking far handsomer than any man Victoria had ever seen. "There. That's better. Lady Victoria, will you come in?"

Victoria, perfectly incapable of meeting anyone's gaze—but most of all the one belonging to the man she'd just been kissing—hurried inside, where she was immediately accused by her aunt, because of her high color, of having caught a chill while out-of-doors, and was summarily sent to bed with a hot brick as soon as she returned home . . . a turn of events that did not dismay her at all, as it happened, since her bed now seemed the only place in London where she was safe from the vagaries of her own heart.

CHAPTER TEN

Victoria stood before the mirror in the bedroom she and Rebecca shared, carefully twirling one strand of brown hair around each of her index fingers, then examining the results. It was not ideal, she supposed, but it would have to do. She didn't have time to wait for Mariah and her curling iron.

"Oh!" Rebecca—still in her dressing gown, her own hair tied up in many brightly colored strips of rag—rolled over on the bed and exclaimed, "Oh, Vicky, you *must* hear this part; it is too romantic."

And before Victoria could protest that she had had her fill of romance, thank you very much, Rebecca read aloud from the letter she had received earlier that morning from the extremely prolific Mr. Abbott:

"'Your lips,'" Rebecca read, "'are like sun-kissed cherries. Your skin, the purest cream. Your hair is gold as honey, and your voice an orchestral dream. . . .'"

Victoria said politely, "Isn't that lovely?" and refrained from asking what an orchestral dream might be.

"He's really a very talented poet, isn't he?" Rebecca rolled over again, this time onto her back, and, holding Mr. Abbott's letter at arm's length, admired the way his manly handwriting looked from afar. "I told him he ought to write a book. A book of poems. He could dedicate it to me. Haven't you always longed to have a book of poems dedicated to you, Vicky?"

Victoria, giving up on her curls, reached instead for her second-best bonnet. It was, a glance out the windows showed her, pouring outside (what else was new?), and she was not about to risk her favorite hat in such a deluge.

"Yes," she replied, without having really heard the question.

"I don't suppose there's any chance of that happening to you, is there, Vicky?" Rebecca glanced slyly in Victoria's direction. "I'm sure Lord Malfrey doesn't write poetry. He's not nearly as cerebral as Charles, is he?"

"Yes," Victoria said absently. "Have you seen my umbrella, Becky? Or did I leave it downstairs?"

"I don't know," Rebecca said. "Should you really be going out, Vicky? After all, you looked to be at death's door just last night. Wherever can you be going, anyway, on such a dreary morning?"

"I've an appointment," Victoria said tersely. "With Lord Malfrey."

"With Lord Malfrey? Well, surely you can change it." Rebecca glanced meaningfully at the windows. "It can't be worth going out in all this."

"It is," Victoria replied, slipping on a pair of gloves. "Believe me."

"I think you're being ridiculous. He'd surely understand if you sent a note to say you'll see him later, when the rain stops. The last thing you want, Vicky, is a red nose on your wedding day, and if you keep up with this, that's surely what you'll get. Come in," Rebecca called, in response to a tap at the door.

Mariah opened the door, then bobbed a curtsy, exactly the way Victoria had taught her.

"Begging your pardon, miss," she said, very respectfully, to Rebecca. "But Captain Carstairs is downstairs, and wishes a word with Lady Victoria."

Victoria did not pause as she stuffed a handkerchief and several spare hairpins into her reticule.

"Tell the captain I am not at home," she said without looking up.

Rebecca laid down her letter and regarded her cousin curiously. "Captain Carstairs? Here so early in the day? And in such weather as this? Vicky, surely it must be something quite important to have brought him out in the rain. You can't not see him."

"Tell Captain Carstairs I'm out," Victoria told Mariah. "And you don't know when I shall return."

Mariah bobbed another curtsy and was about to withdraw when Rebecca stopped her.

"Stay, Mariah," she said, and sat up, her gaze on Victoria. "Vicky, use your head. You can't say you're not here. You're about to go out. Supposing he sees you leave the house?"

"I don't care," Victoria said darkly. "Mariah, tell him I'm in bed with a headache."

This time Rebecca did not attempt to stop the maid, who closed the door quietly behind her instead of banging, as had been her custom until Victoria cured her of it.

"Vicky," Rebecca exclaimed. "You are being very rude about poor Captain Carstairs! Ruder, even, than usual. Did he say something to anger you last night?"

"No," Victoria said, reaching for her pelisse.

"Well, did he . . . did he insult you, then?"

"No," Victoria said, throwing the cape about her shoulders and fastening it.

"Then why won't you see him?" Rebecca wanted to know.

Victoria could not, of course, tell her cousin the truth—that she knew precisely why Captain Carstairs was downstairs so early in the morning on such a rainy day. He had already sent, by first post, a note that had contained only three words . . . but three words that had thrilled along Victoria's every vein, even as she'd quickly crumpled the note and hidden it out of sight beneath the bacon platter:

We must talk.
Yours, J. Carstairs

Victoria had not been surprised to see that the captain's handwriting was exactly like him, bold and commanding.

Well, the captain was in for a very unpleasant surprise if he thought that Victoria was like one of his crewmen, and would meekly do as she was bidden. She didn't know why she'd kissed him the way she had the night before— she had been up virtually all night trying to suss it out— but as far as she was concerned, it was a mystery that could remain unsolved forever. Under no circumstances did she ever plan to "talk" to the captain about it . . . or to anyone else, for that matter.

"Because I'm late enough as it is," Victoria said airily in response to Rebecca's question. "Good-bye."

And then, before her cousin could say another word, Victoria hurried from the room they shared, and tripped down the hall to the servants' staircase, since there was no point in claiming to Captain Carstairs she was in bed with a headache if she was only going to run into him on the front steps.

But it wasn't Jacob Carstairs Victoria very nearly fell over as she was hurrying down the staircase, but her second-eldest cousin, Clara, who was seated on the landing sobbing her eyes out in a fashion that would have put many a Shakespearean actress to shame.

Oh, Lord, Victoria thought, lifting her eyes to the ceiling. Was her work in this family never to be done? Was she forever to go from one to the other of the Gardiners, rescuing them from whatever personal crisis befell them next?

Sighing, Victoria sank onto the landing beside the fitfully sobbing Clara, and said, "Now, Clara, dry your eyes and tell me all about it. I haven't long—there's a carriage waiting—so do try to make it short."

Clara hiccupped, wiped her nose on the back of her hand (prompting Victoria to reach into her reticule and offer her clean handkerchief), and said, "Oh, Cousin Vicky. I . . . I am so afraid I sh-shall never find my one true love."

Victoria nodded. "Well, you are only fourteen, after all," she said crisply. "It isn't as if you haven't time."

"But supposing I n-never meet him?" Clara demanded, her blue eyes very wide and tearfilled. "Or supposing I already met him, and let him get away? Supposing my one true love is Robert Dunleavy? Last week I told Robert Dunleavy that his teeth reminded me of . . . of a cemetery!"

Victoria raised her eyebrows at this. "That was unkind. But how. . . ?"

"Oh, you know," Clara said exasperatedly. "His teeth stick out every which way, like headstones, only inside his mouth."

Victoria nodded. "Well, yes. I think it highly unlikely

Mr. Dunleavy is going to think kindly of you after pointing out something like that to him. However, it is equally unlikely that Mr. Dunleavy is your one true love. Or at least, if he is, you still have several years before you can be qualified as on the shelf, and things get absolutely desperate. It's possible that in the interim, Mr. Dunleavy will have forgotten about your unfortunate remark."

Clara, sniffling, asked, "Cousin Vicky, if I do get to be seventeen or eighteen—you know, Becky's age—and I haven't found my one true love, will you find him for me? The way you did for Becky? Will you, please? It would be such a weight off my mind."

Victoria promised solemnly that she would, and Clara, brightening, dried her eyes and scampered away. Victoria straightened her skirts and started to continue down the stairs, only to find her way blocked just beyond the landing where she'd sat with her cousin by none other than Jacob Carstairs himself!

A Jacob Carstairs who had, evidently, been standing there some time, anticipating her escape. And who'd also evidently overheard the entirety of her conversation with her cousin Clara.

"Robert Dunleavy," he observed dryly, blocking Victoria's way along the narrow staircase with his broad shoulders, "will have five thousand a year and an estate in Devonshire one day. For all that, I would think Clara could learn to overlook his teeth."

It was all Victoria could do to remain upright, she was so startled to find him there. Her heart seemed to have swooped up into her throat, and she had to clutch at the walls on either side of the narrow staircase in order to keep from falling over.

"You!" she exclaimed, beside herself with anger—or so she told herself, anyway. For surely it was only rage—white-hot rage—that was making her knees shake and her cheeks burn. "What are you . . . How dare you . . . Why aren't you in the sitting room, where Mariah left you?"

"Wait in the sitting room like a fool, while you creep out the back door?" Jacob Carstairs grinned at her in a manner she found *most* insolent. "Not likely. I'm not an ass. I knew you'd mutiny. You're the type. Now, why won't you talk to me? And where do you think you're going in all this rain?"

Victoria, furious that now she was going to have to have a confrontation with him before she'd had a chance mentally to prepare for one—she'd spent all night preparing mentally for a confrontation with quite a different fellow—spat, "None of your business! I don't have to tell you anything. You don't own me. Now get out of my way."

Jacob seemed to find her ire highly amusing—which only served, of course, to increase it.

"Far be it from me," he said with a chuckle, "to stand in the path of a busy bee like yourself. I'm certain you are off on some new errand of mercy. Some other innocent maid, perhaps, who needs help finding her . . . how did Clara put it? Her one true love?"

Victoria stood on the step above his, inwardly seething. She was so angry she couldn't think of a word to say.

"Poor Miss Bee," Jacob said. "First Rebecca, now Clara. How are you ever going to find your own true love, when you are so busy helping others find theirs?"

Victoria was not, by nature, a violent creature. But she had really taken all that she felt she could, and his snide remark sent her right over the edge. How could he—how *could* he be so cavalier about it, after what he'd told her about Lord Malfrey the night before?

And so she laid firm hands on Jacob Carstairs's coat front and pushed him against the wall as hard as she could. Then, as he was struggling to find his balance, she brushed quickly past him and ran the rest of the way down the steps, ignoring his cries of, "Lady Victoria!" She was out of the house and safely inside the confines of the Gardiners' carriage before he burst from the house, looking very penitent indeed . . . and, she noted with satisfaction, very wet.

Victoria leaned back against the leather seat, but she could not relax. How could she, knowing the odious task that lay before her? She was deeply unhappy with Jacob Carstairs, because he had managed to completely destroy what little equanimity she had possessed before running into him like that in the stairwell. What was it about that man that managed to discompose her so? She had never met anyone who was as capable as he seemed to be of arousing the worst in her.

Well, she would not think about Jacob Carstairs anymore. She had far more pressing problems at the moment . . . and the primary one was that they were pulling up in front of the house in which Lord Malfrey and his mother were renting rooms for the season.

Victoria took a deep, steadying breath, and reached up to give her curls a last twirl with her gloved fingers. She was not at all happy about what she knew she had to do now. But there was a chance—there was *always* a chance—that Captain Carstairs had underestimated the earl . . . or even that Hugo had learned his lesson, and had grown as a person during the time he'd spent abroad. Maybe he simply hadn't loved Margaret Carstairs. Maybe he—

The coach jerked to a halt, and the Gardiners' footman opened the carriage door for Victoria, and held her umbrella over her as she climbed down from the vehicle, then up the steps to the door.

Lord Malfrey was—as he'd promised to be when Victoria sent her message to him, early that morning—at home. He was even waiting for Victoria in the rented sitting room he and his mother shared. His mother, however, was not there—much to Victoria's relief. She was, his lordship informed Victoria, still asleep. The rain, he said, gave her megrims.

Victoria said she was very sorry to hear it, declined Lord Malfrey's offer of something hot to drink in order to ward off the morning chill, and sat still for a moment on the tuffeted seat he had offered, trying to collect her thoughts. Outside, the rain poured down. Inside the sitting room, with its slightly ostentatious decor, Lord Malfrey seemed attentive as ever, praising her curls, which were, Victoria knew, limp at best, thanks to the weather.

Finally, after gazing at the earl for some time, and wondering how on earth she could ever—ever!—have thought Jacob Carstairs handsome, when Hugo Rothschild was so clearly a superior physical specimen, Victoria summoned her courage, and said, "I'm afraid I've received some very bad news, my lord."

Lord Malfrey, who was picking out a tune on the room's pianoforte, looked unconcerned. "Really, my love? Don't tell me your wedding gown won't be ready on time. I told you to go to Madame Dessange's. Brown's is scandalously overpriced, and never has anything ready in time."

"It isn't my wedding gown," Victoria replied from her chair. She kept her gaze on her gloved hands, folded tightly in her lap. "It's my uncles. I've received a letter from their solicitors, and it contains . . . it contains what I fear might be bad news."

Lord Malfrey looked up sharply from the keyboard, his blue-eyed gaze very penetrating indeed.

"They're well, aren't they?" he asked. "Your uncles?"

Then, with slightly less urgency, "Oh, they're your mother's brothers, aren't they? I'd forgotten."

Victoria winced. This eagerness on Lord Malfrey's part to learn whether one of her uncles was likely to die soon—and possibly leave her yet another inheritance—was not a good sign. Her father, of course, had been the one with the title and fortune. Her uncles had nothing but their military pensions to live upon.

Lord Malfrey, realizing this, looked unconcerned again, and began plunking out another tune, not very well.

"My uncles are fine," Victoria continued with some irritation. Really, this was not going at all as she'd planned. Perhaps she was not acting disturbed enough. Oh, what she'd give for her cousin Clara's ability to produce dramatic tears on demand! "It's just that . . . there's been a terrible mistake."

"A mistake?" Lord Malfrey hit a few more notes. He seemed to be trying to play a rendition of "Pop! Goes the Weasel." "What kind of mistake?"

"Quite a grave one, I'm afraid," Victoria said. "You see, the solicitors have only just discovered that there is a codicil to my father's will."

Lord Malfrey looked up at that. "A codicil? What kind of codicil?"

"Quite a silly one, actually," Victoria said. "You see, my father was terribly overprotective of me, even as a young child, and . . . well, shortly before his death he inserted a codicil to his will that said his fortune was to go to me absolutely . . . but not if I married before I turned twenty-one."

The lid to the pianoforte crashed down, fortunately missing the earl's fingers, but only by a fraction of an inch. He did not appear to notice, however. He sat exactly where he was, staring very intently at Victoria. All of the color seemed to have drained out of his face.

Victoria thought, with a sinking heart, that this was not a good sign.

CHAPTER ELEVEN

Oh, well. She oughtn't have been surprised.

Victoria had been up all night long rehearsing just what, exactly, she'd been going to say to Lord Malfrey. She had not been able to help but fantasize about how he'd respond. In her fantasies, when she'd confessed to Lord Malfrey that she was not entitled to her fortune unless she stayed unwed until she was twenty-one, he, with a manly laugh, had replied that he perfectly understood and would wait until the end of time for her.

And all was well.

But this did not appear to be the way things were going to go in real life.

Victoria had never forgotten a story her ayah had liked to tell her at bedtime when she'd been younger. It had been about a maharaja who so wanted to be sure that his wife loved him for himself alone, and not his riches, that he ordered a hovel to be built some distance from his palace. Then, when he chanced upon an attractive maiden who was not aware of his exalted riches, and thought him only a poor fisherman (they met along the riverbank), he did nothing to disabuse her of the notion. Instead he married her on the spot, and carried her away to his hovel. His bride, not knowing that the man to whom she'd pledged her love was actually a maharaja, was quite happy in the hovel, and cheerfully bore him a half dozen children before her husband finally became convinced of her love for him and broke the news: that he was not, in fact, a fisherman, but the richest man in all of India.

The wife responded by hitting him over the head with a cookpan several times (at least according to Victoria's ayah), so great was her ire that for years they'd struggled on next to nothing when all along her husband had had millions of pounds of gold at his disposal. But eventually she overcame her anger and went with her husband and their children to the palace, where she proved to be a gracious and compassionate ruler, and lived happily for many, many years.

If Lord Malfrey had responded to Victoria's news the way the maiden by the river had, by saying money mattered not to him, and that they would either wait the five years until her fortune became her own, or marry at once and live happily, if impoverished, for the rest of their days, then she'd been quite prepared, unlike the maharaja, to reveal at once that she still had her forty thousand pounds, and that they might dine on champagne and ices for the next fifty years and never know a moment of financial hardship. She wanted to know only that he cared for her a little. Just *a little*.

But she could already tell that Lord Malfrey cared for

her not at all, and that he was not going to say either of those two things—*Let's wait to marry, then,* or *Let's marry at once, and damn the money.* No, Lord Malfrey had grown very pale indeed, and looked the way her uncles had always looked when one of them punched another in the stomach during an argument.

"Twenty-one?" the earl echoed with a gasp. "Can't marry until you're twenty-one? But that's not . . . that's not for another five years!"

"Yes," Victoria said sadly. Sad not because of the five years, but because of Lord Malfrey's expression, which was not encouraging. "Five years *is* a long time. But if one truly loves . . . well, what is five years, or even ten?"

Lord Malfrey, however, did not seem to take so romantic a view of things. He got up from the pianoforte so abruptly that the bench fell over behind him. And he did not even appear to notice. Instead he paced back and forth across the room, dragging his fingers through his golden blond hair, and looking, truth be told, like a man bedeviled.

"How could you not have known this before?" he kept asking. "How could your uncles have kept this from you? It's . . . it's criminal, that's what it is!"

Victoria, watching him, said only, "It's very unfortunate, certainly."

"Unfortunate! It's ridiculous!" Then he stopped pacing, and stared at her. "Was your father a sadist?"

Victoria, who decided she had learned all she needed

to know, gathered up her reticule. "Not to my knowledge, no," she replied. "I suppose he was only hoping to keep me from falling prey to men who might wish to marry me only for my fortune."

Lord Malfrey let out a bitter laugh. "Well, that's one way to do it!" he said.

Victoria stood up. She could not help saying, as she paused to unclasp the buttons on her left-hand glove, "You know, Hugo, many people who have much less to live on than you and I marry and are, by all reports, quite happy."

The earl looked at her in utter disbelief. "*Who?* No one *I* know."

"No," Victoria said. "I would imagine not. No one you know actually works for a living, do they?" Though she knew now that it was a lost cause, she could not help adding, "My uncle Walter might have helped, you know. He could have found you a post in his shipping business."

Lord Malfrey looked incredulous. "*Work?* Victoria, what do you take me for? Do I look like a man who is cut out to work for a living? And in *shipping?*" He heaved a shudder. "The only careers that are at all suitable to a man of my rank are the church and the law, and they both require simply odious amounts of schooling. You know I am not bookish."

"No," Victoria said. "You aren't, are you?" She pulled off her glove and removed the ring with the emerald stone that he had given her. She wondered, vaguely, how he was going to pay for it, since she was now quite sure the story he'd told her about his family portraits was untrue, and that he'd bought the ring on credit, thinking he'd pay for it with her money once they were wed. "Well, this is good-bye, then, Hugo. Or should I say, Lord Malfrey."

He looked dully at the ring as she placed it on the lit-tle table by her chair. He did not deny that was the end of their relationship. He did not even bother to say he was sorry for it. She could not help wondering if he'd been more civil to Margaret Carstairs. She was somewhat sur-prised Jacob hadn't gone after him with a fire poker. But she supposed the earl had left town before the captain had gotten the chance.

"And there isn't anything you can do?" Lord Malfrey asked in a plaintive voice. "Any way you can . . . I don't know. Reason with them?"

"With my father's solicitors, you mean?" She looked at him blankly as she pulled her glove back on. "Reason with them about what?"

"The will! Your father's will! There's got to be a way around that codicil, hasn't there?"

The door opened, and the dowager Lady Malfrey came into the room, wearing a white lace cap upon her head and dressed in a robe splendiferous with maribou that was at least two sizes too small for her round frame.

"What codicil?" she asked, holding a glass of what

appeared to be ice water against one temple. "Good morning, Lady Victoria, and forgive me for my late rising. I have quite a megrim. How I hate all this rain! What codicil, my love?"

As the dowager sank down into the seat Victoria had just vacated, her son exploded, "Mama, Victoria's made an awful discovery. There's a codicil to her father's will that she loses her fortune if she marries before her twenty-first year!"

The dowager Lady Malfrey turned her blue eyes—which Victoria now saw were not good-humored at all, but actually filled with shrewish malice—upon her son's former fiancée.

"What's this?" she demanded in a voice that rose in pitch and fervor with her words. "Can't marry until your twenty-first year? But that's five years from now!"

Victoria refrained from remarking that, for people who professed a lack of bookishness, the arithmetic skills of both mother and son were exemplary.

"That is correct," Victoria said.

"And you've waited until *now* to tell us," the dowager exclaimed, "when the invitations are already at the engravers?"

"You needn't worry about that," Victoria said lightly. "I sent a note to the engravers this morning."

"Well, that's a relief," the dowager said. Then her shrewish glance grew suspicious, and she eyed Victoria very closely indeed. "Wait a minute. You sent the engravers a note this morning? Just when did you learn of this codicil of your father's, my lady? 'Tis only just gone past half after nine! What lawyer's offices open for business at such a barbaric hour?"

Victoria smiled pleasantly at the dowager. "How perceptive you are, madam," she said. Then, turning toward Lord Malfrey, she said, "My dear Hugo, I cannot continue this facade. There is no codicil. I lied to you just now. My fortune is my own, as it always has been."

Lord Malfrey stared at her for a moment. Then a look of great happiness spread across his handsome features.

"A joke!" He looked ready to burst with relief and joy. "It was all a joke! Oh, Vicky! How rich!"

But the dowager Lady Malfrey's gaze was upon the emerald ring in the center of the little table before her.

"Joke?" she echoed. She lifted her gaze and sent a piercing look in Victoria's direction. "It wasn't a joke at all, was it, Lady Victoria?"

"No, my lady, it wasn't." Victoria did not know how she stood there before them as tall and as straight as she did. Her knees were shaking, and disappointment was causing her throat to ache.

Stronger, however, than her disappointment was Victoria's shame in herself. She could not believe she had been so easily—and completely—duped. For a part of her had truly believed that Jacob Carstairs was wrong, and that

Hugo Rothschild had loved her—had loved her from the moment he'd first seen her, as he'd assured her that night in the moonlight on the deck of the *Harmony*, when he'd proposed. A part of her had truly believed that the earl would have done anything—even become employed—for her. It was truly the hardest blow she'd ever been dealt in her life—worse even than losing her parents, since she so dimly remembered them—learning that Hugo Rothschild didn't care a jot for her.

But it was better—far better, she told herself—to have found out now, before the wedding, than after. Now she was ashamed, it was true. But she was more or less unscathed. Had she found out about Lord Malfrey's true nature after the wedding, though . . . well, she'd have been trapped in a loveless marriage.

At least this way she was free. Free to walk out that door and marry whomever she liked.

Only . . . who? For the only other man who had ever made her heart skip a beat, as Lord Malfrey had, was a man she despised with every fiber of her being . . .

. . . as well as the man to whom she owed thanks for her present state of utter wretchedness.

"I had hoped, Lord Malfrey," Victoria said, tears—as yet, she was thankful, unshed—of wounded dignity making her voice unsteady, "that you did not care solely for my fortune, and that you loved me at least a little. But I can see now that I was mistaken in that hope. Please consider our engagement at an end, and do not attempt to contact me ever again. I hope you will understand if I see myself out, and do not wait for your servant. Good morning."

Victoria turned to go, but was unfortunately not quick enough to escape Lord Malfrey's impassioned plea that she give him another chance—that of course he loved her, only he was so stunned by the news she'd imparted that he hadn't expressed himself the way he'd meant to. Nor did she manage to slip out in time to miss the dowager Lady Malfrey's fainting fit.

And Victoria being Victoria, she was perfectly incapable of simply walking away when there was a creature in need. And so instead of exiting icily, as she'd intended, Victoria rang for the dowager's maid and stayed at the unfortunate lady's side, chafing her wrists and pressing hartshorn upon her, until aid in the form of a rather slatternly-looking abigail arrived. Sadly, this also meant that Victoria was forced to listen to Lord Malfrey's apologies that much longer.

They were, so far as apologies went, eloquent and impassioned. But they did nothing to dissuade Victoria from, once the young man's mother regained consciousness, repeating her good-byes and departing with as much haste as she could.

It was only when she was seated at last in the Gardiners' chaise-and-four and on her way home again that

Victoria gave herself permission to cry. . . .

But of course when she was finally willing to allow herself to weep, she found that she could not. Though her
throat ached mightily, her eyes were perfectly dry. She rode
home in a state of shock, unbetrothed and unwanted,
unable to cry and yet seething inside. It was bad luck for
Captain Carstairs that he happened to be the first person
Victoria encountered upon setting foot back inside the
Gardiners' door.

"What?" she demanded rudely, seeing him coming
down the hallway with Jeremiah and Judith riding upon his
back, peacock feathers in their hands to serve as switches.
"*You're* still here?"

"I thought I made myself clear," Captain Carstairs said,
with a smile she supposed other girls might find charming,
but which she found only insufferably roguish. "We simply have *got* to talk, Miss Bee."

That was the final straw. Victoria could take many
things—the foul weather, her hair's refusal to curl, even
betrayal by the man to whom she'd pledged her heart. But
she couldn't, simply couldn't take being called Miss Bee on
today, of all days.

And so, uttering a prolonged and heartfelt scream, she
barreled past Captain Carstairs and two of her very surprised cousins, and ran up the stairs to her room, where
she astonished Rebecca by diving beneath the covers of her
bed and refusing to come out from under them for the rest

of the day, despite continued entreaties by Rebecca, Mrs. Gardiner, Mariah, and even Clara, who brought the unwelcome news that Lord Malfrey was below, and wished a word.

It was only then that Victoria, still in her bonnet, lifted her head and conveyed the unhappy truth: that her wedding to the earl was off, and that she would appreciate it if everyone were to leave her alone for the rest of the day.

The Gardiners, stunned but sympathetic, did as Victoria bade. She was left alone, with only Mariah to hover about and ask if she could bring her ladyship anything, such as ices or back copies of the *Ladies' Journal*, which were, Mariah confided to Cook, the sorts of things she herself would want, if *her* man had up and left her.

Lord Malfrey was sent away with looks of great suspicion and mistrust, since the Gardiners did not know it was their niece, and not the earl, who'd broken off their engagement.

Only Captain Carstairs, hearing the news from a very agitated and happy Clara (who dearly loved tales of gloom and heartbreak, particularly any that involved her female relations), seemed unsurprised, and said only that he hoped Lady Victoria felt better upon the morrow, when he would return to call upon her. Then he went home whistling, to Clara's great disapproval, in spite of the rain, the solemnity of the occasion, and the fact that gentlemen simply did not whistle.

In fact, Clara later informed her sister, it was a very good thing she had transferred her affections from Captain Carstairs to Mr. Abbott, because Uncle Jacob, Clara confided, seemed rather *insensitive* . . . a sentiment with which Rebecca, in light of the whistling, was forced to agree.

CHAPTER TWELVE

After such an ignominious end to her engagement to Lord Malfrey, Victoria by rights could have spent the rest of the following week in bed, and no one would have thought ill of her. A girl who'd suffered a broken engagement for whatever reason——whether she had broken it off herself, or her former fiancé had called it quits——was a piteous girl indeed, and there wasn't a matron in London who wouldn't have understood if Victoria quietly withdrew from society for the rest of the season.

But Victoria simply had too much to do to spend more than twenty-four hours wallowing in her own grief. After all, she had all of her wedding plans to cancel, not to mention Rebecca's romance with Charles Abbott to coordinate. And then there were the younger Gardiners, who, by her catching them at such a tender age, might be molded by Victoria into respectable citizens of the commonwealth. Clara needed to be taught that dramatics were all well and good in their place, but that that place was nowhere outside of the schoolroom. And young Jeremiah still, upon occasion, lifted the household pets, and oftentimes his little brother, by the head, a habit of which Victoria was determined to cure him.

Mrs. Gardiner—though she might not be aware of it—needed Victoria's help in keeping the household running smoothly, and Mr. Gardiner had, through Victoria's careful tutelage since her arrival, actually begun saying things other than "Harumph" at the dining table. He was, Victoria felt confident, just days away from actually uttering a whole sentence about something other than the food. To quit now would be, in Victoria's mind, as catastrophic as the floods that sometimes swept through the Indian villages near which she'd grown up, killing hundreds and leaving just as many homeless.

Victoria simply couldn't give up on any of these projects at so crucial a stage, and so was up and out of bed the next morning, with eyes still devoid of redness—for even in the dead of night, when the thought struck her like a knife that she was unattached again, and would have to start all over if she ever wanted to get married, she had not been able to shed a tear.

She refused, however, to worry about this seeming coldness on her part. The loss of Lord Malfrey, she told herself, was so profoundly distressing that she couldn't even weep over it. No, it was clear that inside her chest, her heart was weeping blood. . . .

But she kept this picturesque image to herself, lest Clara overhear it and attempt to employ it during her next impassioned speech about her having not yet discovered her one true love.

Victoria had other things to deal with besides the Gardiners and the cancellation of her wedding plans. No, there was a certain pesky ship captain who kept appearing on her aunt and uncle's doorstep, demanding to see her. Victoria had, upon waking the morning after her sad parting of ways from Lord Malfrey, penned a quick note to Captain Carstairs in response to the one she'd received from him the day before. Her note was almost as brief as his had been. It said:

> *Nothing to talk about. Kindly leave me alone.*
>
> *Yours, V. Arbuthnot*

Victoria could not, for the life of her, make out which part of *Kindly leave me alone* Jacob Carstairs did not understand, but these four words were apparently as foreign to him as Hindustanee, since he showed up at the house shortly after receiving her missive, and would not leave, according to a distraught Mrs. Gardiner, until he'd seen the Lady Victoria.

"I know you're hardly in the mood for company, Vicky," her aunt Beatrice said, as Victoria sat at that good lady's secretary in the morning room, dashing off letters to her bank—for though she felt sorely used by Lord Malfrey, she *had* been stupid enough to agree to marry him at one point, and so she thought it only fair to pay for such expenditures as the picnic (it was not, after all, the dowager's fault her son was a cad), and was directing her agents to send checks to cover whatever bills the Rothschilds might have accrued in her name. The only thing for which she swore she would not pay was that ring. That, she felt, had been Hugo's folly, for which he alone must pay . . . just as she would, from now until the end of time, have to pay for ever having entertained the idea of marrying him in the first place.

"But," Mrs. Gardiner went on, "Captain Carstairs is . . . well, like part of the family. And he does look rather . . ."

Here the good woman sent a piercing look in her eldest daughter's direction, but seeing Rebecca gnawing on the tip of her own pen—for she was absorbed in responding to a letter from Mr. Abbott, and was trying to think of a word besides *deplorable* that rhymed with *adorable*—decided that it was safe to continue.

"Well, he seems *eager* to see you," Mrs. Gardiner went on. "Don't you think you could just poke your head in and tell him you're all right? Because he says he won't leave until he's had a word, and yesterday, you know, he was here for seven hours—"

Victoria threw down her pen and rose with a sigh.

"Very well, Aunt," she said, feeling very irritable indeed. She had no idea what game the captain was playing, but she supposed it had something to do with that kiss—that horrid, wretched, wonderful kiss—that she had been trying ever since to put out of her head, without much success. If Lord Malfrey had ever kissed her like that, she supposed she would not have minded in the least that he was only marrying her for her money, so long as he kept on kissing her that way, and on a regular basis.

But as it had been the odious Jacob Carstairs, and not the earl, who'd kissed her with so much passion and abandon, she could only feel agitated over the entire situation.

Victoria left the morning room and went down to the drawing room, where the captain had installed himself to wait for her. She walked in to find him swinging his arms like a gorilla in front of some of the smaller Gardiners, and uttering what she supposed he figured were apelike sounds. His audience sat in rapt and wide-eyed silence before him, until one of them noticed Victoria in the doorway and said, "Look, Cousin Vicky! Uncle Jacob is a monkey!"

"He most certainly is," Victoria said, as Jacob straightened and, not even looking sheepish, shooed his audience——bitter in their disappointment that the show was over——away.

When they were finally alone, Jacob Carstairs pulled on his waistcoat——not that it did any good: his collar points stayed exactly where they were, still at least two inches lower than any other man's in England——and, without bothering with social niceties such as "good morning" or "Lady Victoria, you look a vision of loveliness"——said,

"Well. Is it true? Have you chucked him?"

Victoria raised her gaze to the ceiling. Really, she did not know why she constantly had to be stuck with such incompetent suitors. Either they were only interested in her for her money, or they seemed simply to have no idea how rational human beings conducted themselves. She said tiredly, "If you mean by that very rude question has my engagement to Lord Malfrey been called off, the answer is yes, it has."

And then, seeing with horror that an extremely self-satisfied smile was creeping across the captain's face, Victoria added hastily, "And kindly do not think that anything you said—or did—to me the other night had anything whatsoever to do with my decision to end my relationship with him. I merely had occasion to observe that he was not quite as . . . honorable as I might have hoped."

"Occasion to observe." Sadly, Jacob Carstairs was still smiling. "And precisely how did this *occasion* arise?"

"Never you mind," Victoria said severely, her heart beginning to thump in a most unsatisfactory manner. Jacob Carstairs was the very last person on earth whom she wanted to know the truth about how she'd tricked her former fiancé into revealing his true colors. Why was it that she could never seem to maintain an air of ladylike refinement around this man, of all men?

"Suffice it to say," Victoria went on, "that it did. And now that Lord Malfrey is gone from my life, you haven't any reason to bother with me. I hope you will . . . well, go and bother the next poor heiress he gets himself engaged to." She turned around and went to the door to the drawing room, pointedly holding it open for him. "Good day, Captain."

But Captain Carstairs didn't budge from where he stood before the drawing room windows—through which sunlight, a rather strange sight after so much rain, filtered shyly, bringing out light brown highlights in his otherwise dark hair. Instead of leaving, however, he merely grinned at Victoria.

"I don't have any reason to bother with you, do I?" he asked, with one rakishly raised eyebrow. "Is that what you *really* think, Miss Bee?"

Furious—because one of the parlor maids, polishing the newel post at the bottom of the staircase to the second floor, overheard the captain calling Victoria Miss Bee, and looked extremely surprised by the impertinence—Victoria slammed the door closed again, shutting out the maid, and whirled upon the captain with blazing eyes and even hotter cheeks.

"Now see here," she said in a hiss. "I did what you said! I got rid of him—the man I loved!—because you told me he was a rogue, and, as it happened, this one time you were right. But that does not, by any stretch of the imagination, mean that I am about to welcome romantic attentions from the likes of *you.*"

Jacob looked unimpressed by this speech. In fact, he did not even appear to have heard the latter part of it. He said merely, and with supreme confidence, "You didn't love him."

"I most certainly did, too!" Victoria cried, stamping her foot the way Jeremiah did when he wanted more dessert and Victoria wouldn't allow him any.

"No, you didn't." Jacob Carstairs shook his head. "You were drawn to him because he needed you, and you can't resist anyone in need. But that isn't love."

Victoria, blinking as if he'd slapped her, thought of the way she'd lain awake in the middle of the night, perfectly unable to weep over losing the earl. Was it possible Captain Carstairs was right? Was it possible she had never loved Lord Malfrey after all, and that was why she hadn't shed a tear over him?

Before she had a chance to think this over, the captain strode across the room until he stood just a foot away from her. Then, looking down into her upturned face, he said, "What you've got to do now is find someone who doesn't need you, and marry him."

Victoria, entirely more conscious than she cared to be of Jacob Carstairs's mouth, which was just inches from hers, tore her gaze from it, and tried to think of nothing but her dudgeon over the captain's impertinence.

"And what," she inquired, looking at the picture frame just behind Jacob Carstairs's head, "would be the point of my doing that, pray?"

"Everyone around you," Jacob Carstairs said, "needs something or other from you. Your aunt needs your help managing her unruly brood and her incompetent cook, your cousin Rebecca needs your help in navigating the tricky waters of her romantic life, your uncle needs your help in keeping him from turning into a harumphing automaton, the footpads of London need your help in avoiding the gallows. Wouldn't it be restful, Miss Bee, if, after a long day of flitting about and helping people, you could come home to someone who needed nothing whatsoever from you?"

Victoria stared up at him, perfectly incapable of making out just what, exactly, he was trying to say. It almost sounded—but surely not—as if he were . . .

Well, proposing.

But that, of course, was impossible, because first of all there was no moonlight; secondly, he was not even touching her; thirdly, she had yet to hear anything like a romantic sentiment from him, such as "Victoria, I can't live without you," or "If I don't have you, I shall go mad"; and lastly, it was *Jacob Carstairs*. And Jacob Carstairs would never ask Victoria to marry him. Why, he was forever teasing her, calling her Miss Bee, and making light of her deadly serious attempts to improve the lot of others!

Not to mention the fact that she had, up until recently, been engaged to the man who had broken the heart of his elder sister.

"I don't . . . "Victoria, for perhaps the first time in her entire life, could not think how to respond to the captain's very unorthodox proposal . . . if proposal it even was! She was still not entirely sure.

Feeling muddled, she said only, "I can't say I agree with you, Captain. I don't . . . I don't think it would be restful at all." And thinking of Jacob Carstairs's well-appointed town house, his competent, intelligent mother, and superior household staff—she doubted tureen of beef had ever once been served at the Carstairses' dining table—she added with feeling, "In fact, I think it would be dull. Very dull, indeed!"

"Dull?"

And now he *was* touching her! He'd reached out and lifted one of her hands in his, and she wasn't wearing any gloves, and neither was he! She could feel the calluses on his fingers—his being a man who worked for a living, even if now he was handling more of the administrative concerns of his business than actually lifting rigging and tying off sails, she supposed Jacob *would* have calluses. Lord Malfrey, of course, hadn't had any, because he'd always worn gloves while riding or doing anything else athletic, such as fencing.

Somehow the feel of Jacob Carstairs's calluses made Victoria's heart slam harder than ever against the inside of her chest.

"I don't think it would be a bit dull," the captain said in a voice she had never heard him use before. She realized, as she watched his fingers entwine themselves with hers, that it was a voice entirely devoid of teasing, or anything at all that might be construed as vexing or snide. *Why*, she thought with some surprise, *he's being serious!*

"In fact," he said, still in that same deep, serious voice, "I think it would be very exciting to be married to someone who doesn't need you, but only . . . wants you."

On the word *wants*, Jacob gave her hand a gentle pull, and Victoria found herself, against all reason, in his arms. How on earth this should have happened *again*, when she had instructed herself very firmly not to let it, she could not imagine.

But there it was, and there came his lips down over hers, and there was nothing, absolutely nothing Victoria could do about it, short of kicking him in the shins and running away, something that, once his mouth was on hers, she was perfectly incapable of doing. Because his lips felt so very *nice* on hers—or rather, not nice. Not nice at all. The *opposite* of nice . . .

Oh, why was this happening to her? She had just escaped a romantic entanglement. She could not throw herself into another so soon. . . .

And yet the captain's lips felt so very right on hers! His arms, going around her, made her feel so very safe and secure, so warm and—yes, there was no denying it— wanted. Not needed, but wanted, a sensation that was as alien to Victoria as, well, poverty. Jacob Carstairs wanted her! Not needed her——what on earth would a man like him need from a girl, even a girl with such very definite opinions on the height at which one's collar points ought to be worn, like her?

No, he wanted her, and that was, Victoria was becoming convinced, even better than being needed. Except . . .

Except that he hadn't actually proposed. He hadn't actually said, "Victoria, light of my heart, will you be my bride?" No, all he'd said was something about "someone," but he had not specified one iota whether or not that "someone" was him. Furthermore . . . furthermore, how dared he stand and kiss her in her aunt and uncle's drawing room without even a proper proposal first?!

Victoria, though it took every ounce of self-control she possessed——for being kissed by Jacob Carstairs was quite the most exciting thing that had happened to her since . . . well, the last time she'd been kissed by Jacob Carstairs——laid both hands upon the captain's chest, and pushed him with all her might.

Jacob staggered backward and almost fell into Mrs. Gardiner's stuffed bird collection, which she kept under bell jars by the pianoforte. He regained his balance just in time, however, and demanded, with a look of shock on his face that was so pronounced it was almost comical, "What the—— Victoria, what did you do *that* for?"

"I might well put the same question to you," Victoria said, trying to ignore her wildly beating heart and a pair of lips that still tingled from the impassioned way his mouth had moved over hers. "You come here, teasing and insulting me—"

"Insulting you?" Jacob cried, looking more shocked than ever. "Victoria, don't be an idiot. I want to marry you!"

"Well, you have a fine way of showing it," Victoria retorted. "Calling me an idiot, and Miss Bee—and in front of the maid, no less!"

"You *are* an idiot," Jacob said firmly, "if you think my calling you Miss Bee is an insult."

"Well, it's hardly a compliment!" Victoria shouted.

Jacob, however, did not shout back at her. Instead he said in a very even, reasonable tone, "Victoria, I'm warning you. You had better stop arguing and accept me now, because I'm not going to ask you to marry me again."

"You never asked me at all!" Victoria cried. "All you said was that it would be very exciting for me if I married 'someone' who wanted me, instead of needing me. You were not, I would like to add, at all specific as to who that *someone* might be!"

"Well, who do you think?" he demanded. When Victoria said nothing, but only stood with her arms folded across her chest, staring stonily into the corner, he said, "For God's sake, Victoria. I'm not going to start extolling your virtues and prattling on about how unworthy I am of you, if that's what you're waiting for. You already got a proposal like that once, and look how it turned out."

Victoria, furious now, turned to him and screamed, "Thanks very much for reminding me! Now get out!"

A look of mingled exasperation and disgust passed across Jacob Carstairs's handsome features. The next thing Victoria knew, he was in the doorway, collecting his hat and gloves from Perkins, the butler, who was pretending he noted nothing amiss between Victoria and her guest.

"You know, Victoria," the captain said just before he shut the door behind him, "you might be interested in knowing that there *is* someone who is very much in need of your guidance . . . someone whose life needs managing far more, I think, than Rebecca's or your precious earl's ever did."

Victoria, thinking he must mean some orphan he'd encountered on the docks, blinked at him with wide eyes, instantly forgetting their quarrel. "Really?" she asked. "Who is it?"

"You," he said, and slammed the door.

𝒬

CHAPTER THIRTEEN

Victoria refused to admit that she was in the least concerned over what had transpired between Captain Carstairs and herself that morning in the drawing room. Jacob Carstairs was nothing but a rude, insolent, conceited rogue, who hadn't the slightest idea what was good for him and in no way deserved his patient, competent mother. For *that* poor lady Victoria could only sigh. Mrs. Carstairs was going to be stuck with her obnoxious son for the rest of her days. Because Victoria did not think there was a young lady in London who would ever be compelled to marry him. Certainly *she* never would. And *she* was already that season's worst hard-luck case, due to her shattering breakup with Lord Malfrey.

But fortunately for Victoria, the general consensus amongst the matrons was that the only daughter of the Duke of Harrow still had her choice of suitors, being at once rich and passably attractive, despite her somewhat questionable parting with the Earl of Malfrey, and her tendency to criticize her hostesses's household staffs.

Still, despite the number of eager mamas who pushed their sons in her direction, Victoria remained, at least for the first few days after her breakup with Lord Malfrey, and her blowup with Jacob Carstairs, stubbornly solo. She had begun, in fact, to entertain fantasies of never marrying at all. Instead, she'd decided, she would open a hospital—solely for the orphaned and indigent—where she could help scads of people with their medical and romantic problems. She would be busy from morning until night, helping people! A lovelier existence Victoria simply could not imagine.

Reality would, however, intrude upon her private dreams, and a week after her unpleasant interview with Jacob Carstairs—who, true to his word, had not mentioned marriage again, nor (more disappointingly) had he tried to kiss her again—she received a note from the wicked Lord Malfrey. This note, unlike the many others he had sent since Victoria had ended their engagement, did not contain any impassioned pleas that she give him another chance or take him back.

This time Lord Malfrey asked if they could make an exchange of letters—hers for his. As this was standard form in any failed romantic relationship, Victoria agreed, and was piqued when Lord Malfrey then insisted that they make the exchange in person. But Hugo argued that the things he'd written to Victoria during the course of their courtship—the letters and poems he had, she was now fairly certain, plagiarized from other, more talented authors than he—were so highly personal that he did not dare trust them to a servant, much less the post, to deliver. No, an exchange must be made, and must be made personally by the correspondents.

Victoria found this very vexing indeed. She had no time to be making clandestine assignations to exchange letters with former fiancés. For from the dust of her own failed engagement had risen a new one . . . her cousin Rebecca's to the wonderful Mr. Abbott. Mrs. Gardiner was beside herself with joy, and even Uncle Walter hadn't harumphed about it once, and said instead that it was jolly good news. Rebecca was completely incapable of discussing anything but wedding clothes and babies, though Clara was not nearly so enthusiastic, frequently reminding her sister not to count her chickens before they'd hatched, for look how poor cousin Vicky's engagement had turned out!

To drag herself in the midst of all this to some appointment with her former fiancé to make an exchange of what, to Victoria's mind, were nothing but a silly pile of letters was most trying. But Victoria supposed it had to be done, and so at five o'clock a week to the day that she had broken things off with the earl, she met him in Hyde Park—at the very spot, in fact, of their ill-fated picnic. It had seemed to Victoria sensible to pick a public place to meet, but a place where they were not likely to draw attention to themselves—for Victoria knew, even after only having been living there a month, how London's gossips' tongues wagged.

Unfortunately, she had not been able to borrow the Gardiners' carriage to take her on her outing, as Rebecca and her mother had needed it for a trip to Madame Dessanges's, who was to make the bridal trousseau. Victoria had instead engaged a hack. Only after sending it away once she reached the appointed meeting place did Victoria begin to have any reservations about her mission, and that was because the sky overhead had begun to look even more threateningly gray than usual. It would be just her luck to be caught out in the open during a thunderstorm.

On the bright side, however, all of the ink on the letters she and Hugo carried might be washed away, and then Victoria would never have to fear seeing some of the more foolish things she'd written in hers in the *Times* or some other shameful place.

Lord Malfrey was not on time. But then, he had never been on time back when they'd been engaged, eight days earlier. Victoria stood beneath a large chestnut tree, watching the other parkgoers scurry for shelter, as very large drops of rain began to fall around her and the sky rumbled ominously.

She was about to give up the effort entirely and go look for a hack to take her home—if, indeed, any were still available, which she thought unlikely, given the weather—when Lord Malfrey finally appeared on a dapple gray mount.

By that time, however, the heavens had opened, and the downpour become even more than Victoria's very sturdy umbrella could withstand. Lord Malfrey, coming to stand beneath it while his poor horse was pelted with rain, shouted, "We oughtn't stand beneath this tree. There's lightning—"

Even as he spoke, a large bolt of it lit the sky, and thunder cracked. Victoria, who knew the weather was one thing she could not control—yet—ran with him out from beneath the tree and stood in the downpour, the hem of her skirt already smeared with mud, and her curls completely limp.

"My letters, please," she nevertheless shouted at Lord Malfrey, who looked down at her as if she were mad.

"I must get you out of this storm," Lord Malfrey said, glancing about as if, Victoria thought disparagingly, Noah and his ark were going to appear and rescue them. "Where is your carriage?"

"I couldn't get the carriage," Victoria said. The rain was falling sideways now, and the umbrella afforded little protection against its slanting assault. Victoria's skirts were as molded to her legs as the young woman's who'd been at the dowager's picnic . . . though not on purpose. The rain was cold and the wind high. Victoria's teeth began to chatter. "I took a hack. Give me my letters, please."

Lord Malfrey's gaze swept Park Lane—at least, what he could see of it through the deluge. "There are no hacks now," he said. "And I can't leave you in this. Here, come." He ducked out from beneath the umbrella and swung back up onto his mount. "Give me your hand, Lady Victoria, and step onto my boot toe."

Victoria, horrified at the very idea of joining Lord Malfrey in the saddle—or anywhere else, for that matter—said, "I shall do no such thing!"

"Lady Victoria," Hugo said, as the rain plastered his fair hair to his face, "I won't leave you alone in this storm. We can be home and dry in a jig if you would just, for once, be sensible."

Victoria would not have obeyed him for the world if it hadn't been for the fact that at that very moment a violent gust of wind ripped her umbrella from her hands and sent it sailing. She watched helplessly as it was tossed by the storm out of sight. It took only a second or two without the meager protection the umbrella had afforded for her to become wet to the bone.

"Oh," she said in a defeated voice, as lightning again tore through the sky. "All right."

Then, placing her foot on Lord Malfrey's boot toe and giving him her hand, she allowed herself to be pulled into the saddle before him.

The ride from the park to safety was not one Victoria would qualify as pleasant or even memorable, with the exception of its extreme discomfort—the way the rain pelted her face; the smell of wet horse; the hideous embarrassment of having Lord Malfrey's arm around her, keeping her from sliding off his horse's slick shoulders. By the time he set her down, Victoria's relief was so great she did not particularly care where she was, so long as it was out of the rain and away from him.

But alas, as they ran up some steps and toward a door that was thrown open by a maid to receive them, Victoria saw with regret that Lord Malfrey had not, in fact, delivered her to her own home, but to his.

"But this isn't the Gardiners'!" she cried, mightily vexed, as she stood dripping in the hallway and the little maid struggled to close the door against the wind behind them.

"My rooms were closer," Lord Malfrey said, wringing out his wet coattails.

Victoria did not know London well enough to judge whether or not Hugo told the truth. But she was, it had to be confessed, too cold and wet to care very much. Still, a second later, when a door opened, and the dowager Lady Malfrey appeared, looking enviously warm and dry, Victoria began to wish she'd paid better attention.

"Oh, my dears!" the dowager cried, seeing them drenched and dripping in the foyer. "You poor things! I'll have Ellen put a kettle on at once for you. Lady Victoria, come with me; we must get you changed into something dry before you catch your death of cold!"

Victoria, who could not imagine a worse or more embarrassing situation—to be forced to take shelter in the very home of the man whose hand she'd accepted, only to spurn a month later!—followed meekly after the dowager, cursing the day she'd ever agreed to come to this foul country. Did it *ever* stop raining in England? Would she *never* be able to present the ladylike figure before others that she'd have liked to?

And why on this day, of all days, had she worn a white skirt, which was now most likely permanently ruined by all the mud she'd encountered?

Victoria was escorted by Hugo's mother not to her own room, where there might have been a fire, but instead to a spare room, where she was given a blanket and towels and told to disrobe. Her clothes, the dowager Lady Malfrey explained, would be spread before the kitchen fire until they dried. In the meantime she could stay in the bedroom to wait for hot tea and brandy.

Victoria did not want hot tea and brandy. She wanted to go home!

But since she did not, she suppose, want to go home in soaking wet clothes—nor, even less, dry clothes belonging to the mother of the man to whom she'd once been engaged—she did as she was bidden, stripping down to her camisole and pantaloons—which were wet as well, but which she did not feel comfortable taking off in what was, after all, more or less a stranger's house.

Sitting in her damp underclothes, with a blanket around her shoulders, and her hair in wet strands all around her face, Victoria stared miserably out the window.

The rain was still coming down in torrents, and the sky had gone dark as if it were night, though it was surely only just six o'clock in the evening. Occasionally lightning sliced through the sky, and thunder rumbled so loudly the sills rattled. Victoria wondered how long it would take for her clothes to dry enough for her to risk putting them on again. Hours, most likely. She would have to send word to her aunt, telling her what had happened, lest Mrs. Gardiner worry.

Accordingly, Victoria tugged upon the bellpull, and when the same sharp-faced little maid who'd met them in the foyer appeared at the door, she said, "Would you please go and ask her ladyship if I might have pen and paper, so that I can send a message to my aunt letting her know I'm all right and shall be delayed?"

The maid bobbed a curtsy and went away, only to come back five minutes later with the things Victoria had asked for, along with a pot of piping hot tea, some cakes, and the brandy.

Victoria, holding the blanket about her, sipped the tea appreciatively and began to feel immeasurably better. She composed her note to her aunt, then rang for the maid again, and, giving her a coin from her reticule, asked if she would see that the letter was delivered at once to the Gardiners'.

The girl said that she would. Victoria, feeling that she'd done all she could for the moment, laid down upon the bed, because there were no books to read in the plain little room, and nothing else to do. Besides, the tea had warmed her, and Victoria had begun to feel pleasantly drowsy after her terrible ordeal. Listening to the pounding rain and thunder, Victoria closed her eyes, meaning only to nap for a moment. . . .

But when she opened her eyes, she realized at once that something was very wrong. Her room was pitch black, the wick in the lamp she'd lit having guttered and gone out while she'd slept. What was more, the storm had ended, and moonlight streamed brightly through the spare bedroom's windows. A swift glance at the ormolu clock on the mantel showed Victoria that she'd been asleep for nearly four hours. It was close to ten. Surely her clothes were, by now, completely dry. Why had the dowager let her sleep so long?

Wrapping the blanket about her now dry underclothes, Grecian toga style, Victoria yanked on the bellpull. She relit the lamp and looked outside. The bedroom in which she'd been placed was on the second floor. Below her she could see the quiet street shining wetly in the moonlight. A few branches had been knocked down during the storm, and lay strewn about. She wondered where her umbrella had ended up.

A tap at the door brought Victoria to it. She opened it to find, somewhat to her surprise, the dowager Lady Malfrey, and not the maid, in the hallway.

"Oh, good evening, madam," Victoria said, slightly

embarrassed to be seen wearing only a blanket and her underthings by the woman who was once going to have been her mother-in-law. "I'm afraid I must have fallen asleep. I was wondering, could you have the maid bring up my clothes? For I'm certain they're dry by now, and I really oughtn't to impose upon your hospitality for a moment longer. Oh, and if you could send for a hack, I would be greatly in your debt."

But the dowager, instead of saying, "Certainly, Lady Victoria, I would be happy to," only shook her head, as if she could not quite believe what she was hearing.

Then Victoria saw, rather to her surprise, that the woman was laughing. Except that Victoria, to the best of her knowledge, had not said anything amusing.

"I beg your pardon, Lady Malfrey," she said. "Have I missed a joke?" She glanced up and down the hallway. "Did Lord Malfrey set up bowling pins in the corridor?" For this was something the dowager had bragged about her son having done once on a rainy day.

"Not hardly," the dowager Lady Malfrey said with a chuckle.

"Well . . ." Victoria knitted her brows. "Then may I ask what is so amusing?"

"*You,*" the dowager said, a fat tear trickling out from between the laugh lines at the corners of her eyes. For the dowager Lady Malfrey was by now laughing so hard, she was crying.

Victoria, taken aback, wondered if perhaps the dowager Lady Malfrey had been at the brandy.

"Excuse me?" Victoria asked politely. "But I'm not certain I heard you correctly. Did you say that . . . *I* am amusing?"

"That's right," the dowager said, wheezing a bit now, she was laughing so hard.

Victoria, who still did not see anything particularly funny about the situation, said rather sharply, "Lady Malfrey, I don't believe you are well. Would you like to come in and have a seat? Or perhaps I could get you a glass of water? For I fear you are not yourself."

"Oh, I feel fine," the dowager said, straightening and dashing away tears of laughter from her eyes. "It's *you* who's not going to feel so well when you realize . . . when you realize . . ."

She was off again, laughing uncontrollably.

"When I realize what, Lady Malfrey?" Victoria demanded very tartly indeed. For she was growing tired of Hugo's mother's antics.

"That you're not going anywhere!" the dowager cried, slapping her knee.

Victoria looked down at the woman, who was now doubled up with convulsive laughter.

"Lady Malfrey," she said severely. "I most certainly am going somewhere. I am going home, just as soon as someone brings me my clothes."

"That's just it," Hugo's mother cried. "That's just it! No one's going to!"

Victoria stared at her. "Whatever do you mean?"

"No one's going to bring you your clothes," the dowager Lady Malfrey said, seeming finally to get some semblance of control over herself. "At least, not until morning."

Victoria, very perplexed by all this, said, "Not until morning? Why ever not? Surely they're dry by now."

"Oh, they are," Hugo's mother said. "They are. But you'll not be given them until morning."

"But . . ." Victoria peered curiously at the older woman. "But why not?"

"Because," the dowager Lady Malfrey said, slipping a lace handkerchief from the sleeve of her gown and applying it to the corners of her eyes, which were still damp with laughter. "You're to spend the night. You can have your clothes in the morning, when the damage is already done."

Victoria still didn't understand. "Damage? What damage? And I cannot spend the night, Lady Malfrey, though your invitation is very kind."

"Oh, for the love of God!" cried the dowager Lady Malfrey, not laughing at all now. "Are you dense, girl? I'm not inviting you to spend the night! I'm keeping you here overnight so that your reputation's ruined, and you'll have no choice but to marry my Hugo!"

Victoria blinked. "But . . . I don't understand. Why on earth should I *have* to marry your son?"

"After disappearing all night with him, then being found next morning, without your clothes on, in his rooms?" The dowager let out an unpleasant cackle. "You'll *have* to marry him, all right."

CHAPTER FOURTEEN

Victoria thought that perhaps Hugo's mother had suffered a fall and struck her head against something. There really was no other explanation for the very odd things she was saying.

"Lady Malfrey," Victoria said as slowly and as patiently as she was able. "Are you quite sure you haven't fallen down? And hit your head on a piece of furniture? Or the stairs, perhaps? I do think I'd better send for a surgeon—"

"Good Lord." The dowager Lady Malfrey glared at Victoria. "Can you really be as stupid as that? Don't you know what's happening to you, child? You're alone, in a man's house, half-naked. And no one knows where you've disappeared to."

Victoria shook her head. "Lady Malfrey, that simply isn't true. My aunt and uncle know exactly where I am. They know that Hugo and I got caught in the rain, and that I came to your rooms to dry off."

"No, they don't," the dowager said.

"Yes, Lady Malfrey, they do. Because I sent them a . . ."

Victoria's voice trailed off as she noticed the piece of folded parchment Hugo's mother now shook from her sleeve. It was the note she had written, hours ago, to her aunt.

"You . . ." Victoria shook herself. She could not quite believe what her eyes were telling her. "You didn't send my note to my aunt?"

"No," the dowager said with a grin that revealed all of her teeth . . . which, while even, were rather gray in color. "No, I didn't send your note to your aunt."

Victoria glanced at the clock on the mantelpiece. The hands pointed at ten after ten.

"But," Victoria said dazedly, "she'll be terribly worried by now, wondering where I've got to. She might think . . . she might think I've suffered an accident or something."

"She might," the dowager said. "And come morning, she'll probably send someone—your uncle perhaps—to come here looking for you."

Slowly—very slowly—Victoria began to realize what was happening.

"And my uncle will find me," she said through lips that had begun to felt numb . . . and, sadly, not because Jacob Carstairs had been kissing them. "He'll find me here, half-naked. . . ."

"With my son," the dowager said with another broad grin. "What do you think he will have to say to that, my lady? I can't imagine it will be anything good. No, nothing good at all. In fact, I'll wager your uncle'll demand the two of you wed on the spot. Don't you?"

Victoria felt as if something were clutching at her

throat—rather the way she felt when one of the younger Gardiners demanded a piggyback ride down the stairs, then held her in a stranglehold all the way down.

"But surely . . ." Victoria shook her head, as if trying to clear it. "Surely when I tell my uncle the truth . . ."

"He might even believe you," the dowager Lady Malfrey said with a shrug of her plump shoulders. "Who knows? But even if he does, it won't matter. No one else will, you see. There'll be talk. You won't be welcome at Almack's anymore . . . or anywhere else where polite society gathers. . . . It really was very obliging of you to agree to meet my son, and even more obliging of the weather to rain. Not that it would have mattered if it had stayed dry. He'd have found a way to get you here someway or other."

Victoria stared at Hugo's mother in horror. She could not believe what was happening. It was like something out of one of the books Rebecca was always reading, the ones she kept under her bed and that Mrs. Gardiner knew nothing about, in which innocent young maidens were ravished by foreign gentlemen or held captive in pirate caves.

Only this was no book! This was really happening, and not to an innocent young maiden, but to Victoria! Lady Victoria Arbuthnot!

Granted, there were no foreign gentlemen involved, and certainly no pirates. But Hugo's mother's plan was diabolical just the same! Why, the woman intended to hold her captive overnight, and make out in the morning that

Victoria had stayed there willingly for some sort of romantic tryst with Lord Malfrey.

When word got out (and it would; the dowager would see that it would) that Victoria and the earl had spent the night together alone—for the dowager would be sure to let Mr. Gardiner know that she had not been home—Victoria would have no choice but to marry the earl . . . marry him or be branded a scarlet woman, a hussy, a . . .

Victoria, instead of fainting like the heroines of Rebecca's favorite novels usually did, demanded of her captress rather sharply, "Where's Hugo?"

The dowager Lady Malfrey did not look at all miffed by Victoria's tone. She replied, affably enough, "He's next-door. And if you're hoping to appeal to his gentlemanly nature, don't bother. This was all his idea."

Victoria simply did not believe the dowager. She said, "I want to see him. Send him to me now."

The dowager laughed. "You, my dear, are hardly in a position to be making demands. And may I remind you to whom you are speaking? I am going to be your mother-in-law. You had best start treating me with the respect I am owed. After all, once you are married to my son, your fortune will be his."

Victoria realized, with a sinking heart, that what the dowager said was true. Sadly the law dictated that any wealth or property a woman possessed became, upon her wedding day, her husband's.

Which was why Victoria suddenly shouted, "I'd sooner die than marry that poncey git!" and thrust an extremely unladylike elbow into the dowager's clavicle.

Then, while Hugo's mother struggled to catch her breath, Victoria started barefoot down the hallway—for she had given up her shoes, as well, to have the mud scraped from them—intent upon finding her clothes, donning them, and leaving this horrible house forever.

Sadly, however, she did not get very far. A door opened, and none other than the ninth Earl of Malfrey himself emerged from behind it, looking not a little surprised to see Victoria bearing down upon him in nothing but her underclothes and a blanket.

"Here, here," Hugo said, catching Victoria by the arm as she attempted to dart past him. "Where do you think you're going?"

"I'm going home," Victoria said, twisting to be free of his hold. "And if you dare to try to stop me, I'll . . . I'll call the Bow Street Runners on you!"

"I'm certain you would if you could," Hugo said with a laugh. "But I don't think they'll be able to hear you calling from here."

Victoria, struck to the core by this betrayal, narrowed her eyes at him and said, "It's true then. You *are* on her side."

Lord Malfrey glanced at his mother, who was still attempting to recover from the blow Victoria had given her, and was breathing hard and clutching her throat.

"Yes," Hugo said. "Of course. Mama and I are a team—Ah!" The earl snatched his hand out from between Victoria's teeth, which she'd sunk into it with all her might. But he did not, as Victoria had been hoping, release her. He caught her up around the waist instead, lifting her halfway off the floor as she kicked and clawed to free herself.

"Now, Vicky," the earl said with a chuckle. "Don't take on so. I know this is a damnable way to go about it, but you and I were always meant to marry. You know that. There was a time when the idea was hardly repugnant to you. Try to remember—ow, now that *hurt!*— how you used to feel about me, and we ought to get on fine."

As he spoke, the earl half dragged, half carried Victoria back to the spare room. Victoria put up a valiant struggle, but in the end, Hugo—who was apparently immune to pinches, kicks, scratches, and hair pulling—was simply stronger and bigger than she was. He deposited her unceremoniously on the bed, then, before she could beat him to it, flung himself out the door, slamming it hard behind him— even worse, he thought to snatch up Victoria's reticule on the way out, and take it with him. So now she did not even have a hope of bribing a servant to free her! Wretched man.

"Vicky," the earl said from the other side of the door as Victoria fell upon it, beating it with her fists. "Be reasonable. Will being married to me really be such a hardship? We'll have a jolly time, I promise you. And it isn't as if there's some other fellow you like better."

Victoria, upon hearing this last, gave the door a kick with her bare foot that succeeded only in sending jolts of pain up her leg. The door itself didn't budge.

"Vicky," Lord Malfrey chastised her from behind the door. "Really. Is that any way for the daughter of a duke to behave? I do hope you'll have calmed down by breakfast. I'll bring it up to you myself, if you like. One egg or two?"

"Don't"—Vicky went to the mantel and picked up the ormolu clock—"call me"—she threw the clock with all her strength against the door—"Vicky!"

The clock didn't even break. The glass faceplate shattered, but that was all. And behind the door, Lord Malfrey only laughed harder.

"Oh, Vicky," he said. "At least life with you will never get boring."

And then Victoria heard a sound that made her blood run cold—a key scraping in the door's lock.

And that was that. She was locked in. She would not, she knew, be released until morning. Morning, at which point the name Lady Victoria Arbuthnot would be synonymous with . . .

Well, mud.

Perfect. Just perfect. Victoria sank down upon the bed and found that she was trembling. With rage, she told herself. She was weak with it. White-hot rage, not fear. For Victoria was not afraid. She *wasn't*. She . . .

Was. Who wouldn't be? She was trapped in her

undergarments in a stranger's bedroom, and come morning her reputation would be in ruins, her good name worthless.

Well, one thing Victoria knew for certain: she would never marry Hugo Rothschild, no matter what her uncle or anyone else said. She'd sooner go back to India than marry that blackguard, that mountebank, that . . .

. . . rogue.

But even as she told herself that all was not lost—she could, after all, simply say no when the preacher asked if she took this man to be her husband—she realized that if she refused to marry Hugo, it wouldn't be just her own reputation that would suffer. No, the Gardiners would be irrevocably hurt as well. Would Charles Abbott want to marry the first cousin of so brazen a girl as Lady Victoria Arbuthnot? And what of Clara? What were Clara's chances of ever finding her one true love, when her family would lose their tickets to Almack's because of Victoria's refusal to marry the man in whose home she spent a chaperonless night?

It was one thing permanently to destroy her own life. It was quite another to destroy the lives of the people she'd come to love. Yes, love. Victoria loved the Gardiners, for all their faults, from Uncle Walter and his harumphs to Cook and her tureen of beef.

For their sake, she was going to have to marry Hugo.

Victoria felt, for the first time all evening, sick to her stomach.

Marry Hugo! Marry the earl! Only a week before she'd

have laughed giddily at the suggestion. Of course she was going to marry Lord Malfrey! She loved him, didn't she?

But Victoria knew now that what she'd felt for the earl hadn't been love. She had admired him, certainly, for he had cut a very dashing figure on the deck of the *Harmony*. She had been attracted to him, because he was so very handsome, with his blue eyes and golden hair. And she had certainly allowed herself to be flattered by him . . . something at which he'd definitely excelled. Flattering her, that is. Certainly no one else on the *Harmony* had ever bothered to mention her emerald (well, hazel, actually) eyes, or highly kissable mouth. . . .

But love? She had never loved Hugo. She had only said yes to his proposal in the first place because she'd known it would annoy Jacob Carstairs. Yes! She was willing to admit it now, the shameful, horrible truth of it all. She had said yes to Lord Malfrey's proposal because she'd known Jacob Carstairs had overheard it, and that her saying yes would irritate the captain no end.

What kind of reason was *that* to agree to marry a man? Even the most generous of souls would have to agree: an exceptionally poor one.

And what kind of girl did that make her? What kind of girl said yes to a man's marriage proposal because she was hoping it would make another man—yes! Yes, she admitted it!—jealous?

For she had hoped against hope that Jacob Carstairs

would be jealous that she was marrying the earl, and would beg her to marry him instead.

Not that if he had, she'd have done so! Perish the thought! Jacob Carstairs was a thoroughly provoking, completely irascible man, with his *Miss Bees* and his snide remarks and his always thinking he knew better than she did.

And stubborn! The height at which he wore his collar points certainly proved that. The man was impossible, a thorough reprobate. It was ridiculous that his kisses should make her head spin the way they did, ridiculous they should make her so weak at the knees. He was a rogue of the first order, and the last man on earth Victoria would ever consider marrying.

But Victoria would have liked him to have asked her— nicely—just the same.

Sitting on the bed, staring blindly out the window, Victoria wondered what Jacob Carstairs was going to think when he found out about her having spent the night in the earl's rooms. Surely he, of all people, would know that Victoria had been tricked into it. Worse than tricked. Held against her will. Surely Jacob, knowing Victoria as he did, would guess that she would sooner have died than disgrace herself—and her family—in such a way. Surely Jacob . . .

Jacob Carstairs, Victoria realized with growing horror, wouldn't think any such things. He would think she was just a silly girl who'd gotten herself into a silly situation from which she ought to have been able to extricate herself.

She was Miss Bee, after all. Miss Bees did not—simply did not—get kidnapped by earls and held against their will.

Instead, they escaped.

Slowly Victoria's gaze focused on the window she'd been peering blindly out of for so many minutes.

A window. There was a window in her room.

Getting up from the bed, Victoria crossed to the window and laid her fingers over the casement latch. It lifted easily. A second later the window was swinging outward . . .

. . . and the cool night air hit her face, smelling sweetly fresh after the rainstorm. Leaning forward, Victoria looked out. The bedroom in which she was imprisoned was on the far side of the house. Below her lay a garden, dripping and dark. Beyond the garden wall was the street, empty this time of night, and still shining wetly in the moonlight. If she could climb down into that garden, it would be very easy to scale that wall and follow that quiet, narrow street to freedom.

Except . . .

Except that she was in her undergarments. Her undergarments and a blanket. And she was barefoot. Even if she were to find a Bow Street Runner—and Victoria hadn't the slightest idea how one was supposed to go about summoning one—what would they think of her, a blowsy-looking girl with uncurled—uncombed!—hair, wearing nothing but pantaloons, a camisole, and a blanket?

Victoria felt she hadn't any choice but to risk it. Which,

she asked herself, was worse: being found wandering the streets in one's underthings, or being found in the rooms of a man in the early hours of the morning? If her reputation was going to be ruined anyway—and Victoria was by now convinced it was going to be, marriage to the earl or no marriage to the earl—why not have it ruined on her own terms? She would, she knew, forever after be known as the debutante who paraded around Mayfair in her undergarments.

But Charles Abbott, she felt rather strongly, would sooner marry the cousin of *that* girl than the cousin of a girl who spent the night with a man to whom she was not yet wed. . . .

Her course of action decided, Victoria wrapped the blanket, which had come loose during her tangle with Lord Malfrey, more tightly around her body. Then she climbed carefully onto the windowsill and swung her bare feet into the still, damp air . . .

. . . reminding her of another time she'd been forced to make a less than dignified climb down from a dizzying height.

Don't look down, Jacob Carstairs had advised her then, when she'd hesitated atop the rope ladder from his ship, *and you'll be all right.*

Keeping her eyes averted from the ground so far below her, Victoria clung to the sill and lowered her bare foot, feeling for a toehold in the bricks.

And she began to descend.

CHAPTER FIFTEEN

It was not as steep a climb as the one she'd made down the side of the *Harmony*, but it took considerably longer, seeing as how Victoria had to feel for each foothold, and sometimes couldn't seem to find any. Fortunately the building was old and not in the best of repair, or she might have found herself stuck clinging to the side of the building, unable to descend any farther.

But she managed to find a few places where brick and mortar had chipped away, and that, coupled with the occasional ornamental lintel, got her most of the way down. She jumped the rest of the way when she got to a first-floor window and worried someone might glance through it and see her, then raise the alarm. It was no joke, jumping from such a height without shoes to protect her bare feet from the sting of the ground below. But fortunately the rain had softened the earth, and Victoria, instead of breaking both her legs, sank ankle-deep into the thick black mud of someone's rose garden.

Disgusted—particularly since she lost her blanket in the process and had to pick it carefully from the clinging thorns of a nearby rosebush—Victoria pulled her feet from the oozing mud and made her way through the dark garden to the wall that separated it from the neighbors'. There was, she saw to her relief, a door in the center of the wall, and when she turned the wrought-iron latch, she found that it turned easily . . . though not exactly soundlessly. Glancing back over her bare shoulder, Victoria saw that it was unlikely the shriek from the rusty hinges would be overheard. Everyone in Lord Malfrey's rooms appeared to be asleep—at least, very little light showed through the curtains of his sitting room and bedrooms. She might actually be able to make her escape as easily as that. Except for a few scrapes from thorns, and a set of mud-encased feet, she was unhurt.

How angry Lord Malfrey would be in the morning when he unlocked the door to the spare room and found her gone! La, how Victoria wished she could be there to see his face! It would, she was certain, be a picture.

Then Victoria saw something that quite took her breath away: a head, thrust through the window she'd left open! Lord Malfrey's head, she saw at once. Why, he must have come back to the room to check on her! She hadn't a moment to spare. She needed to fly at once, or be caught.

Slipping through the garden door—wincing as its hinges squeaked, for she was certain Lord Malfrey would look that way and spy her—she found herself not, as she'd expected, in the neighbors' backyard, but in a dark and narrow alleyway between the two garden walls. It occurred to her fleetingly that it was just the sort of place rats liked to hang about.

But she thrust this uncourageous thought from her head—she didn't have time to worry about rats. Earls were her immediate problem. Victoria lifted the hem of her blanket and began to run as quickly as she dared in her bare feet—conscious that there might be broken glass—down the length of the alleyway. She ran in the opposite direction that Lord Malfrey had been looking, which was toward the street, since she feared the alley would spill her out onto it before his very eyes.

It was no fun at all, Victoria soon found, running down a dark alley with no shoes, wearing nothing but your underthings and a blanket, in the dead of night after a rainstorm. All manner of things squished hideously beneath her feet. Indeed, she would not let herself even imagine what those things might be. And there were dogs behind the high garden walls on either side of her, dogs that sensed her running by and set up a terrific racket, barking territorially. Lord Malfrey, Victoria was certain, would find her in an instant, based solely on the alarm being raised by the dogs of the neighborhood.

And though the moon shone brightly, this was not necessarily advantageous, since it only made Victoria more conspicuous to anyone who might happen to be looking for her. Worse, it cast large parts of the alleyway in deep shadow . . . shadows from which Victoria could not help imagining all manner of unsavory individuals leaping out and attacking her. Never mind rats or vicious dogs. What about footpads? Or worse, pirates?

Her heart in her throat, Victoria stumbled as quickly as she could down the alleyway. She was approaching, she could see, a street—a blessed street! A street down which hacks rumbled—she saw one go by! Oh, if only she could flag down a hack and take it to her aunt and uncle's house, and to safety. She hadn't any money with her, of course, but she was certain she could convince the driver that he would be handsomely rewarded by her uncle once he delivered her. . . .

Only when Victoria, with a final burst of desperate speed, certain that at any moment the earl was going to spring out from behind her and stop her, finally made it to the street and leaped in front of the first carriage she saw in an attempt to stop it, the driver cursed at her very rudely! Cursed at her, and said it would be a cold day in hell when he'd let one of *her* kind into his nice clean hack!

Victoria, enraged, stared after the hack as it clattered away. One of *her* kind? What ever could the driver have meant? Did he mean the daughter of a duke? But everyone liked dukes' daughters.

Never mind. That particular driver clearly had some sort of problem. Here came another carriage, sadly not a hack, but a very respectable-looking chaise-and-four. Victoria raised her arms and cried to the driver, "Oh, sir, if you please, I'm in terrible trouble. Could you kindly take me to—"

But the driver made a very rude noise and raised his whip at her! Raised his whip and cried, "Out of my way, lassie! I'll have none of your tricks tonight!"

None of her tricks? Victoria, who'd leaped from the path of the carriage—indeed, she'd have been trampled if she had not—blinked after it, stunned to the core. Tricks? What was *wrong* with everyone? Couldn't they see that she was a desperate kidnapping victim and needed immediate rescue? Good Lord, if this kept up Victoria would be out here all night. And surely then Lord Malfrey would find her. . . .

And then from around the corner came a sight so welcome to Victoria's sore eyes, she very nearly giggled for joy. For it was a Runner, a Bow Street Runner, swinging his stick and whistling a happy tune. Victoria, delirious with joy, ran toward him.

"Oh, sir, sir," she cried when she reached his side. "I am so happy to see you! You must help me, sir. My name is Lady Victoria Arbuthnot, and there's been a terrible—"

"Get on with you, miss," the Runner said affably enough, giving her a gentle push away from him. "This is a nice neighborhood. Get on back to Seven Dials, where you belong."

Victoria, stunned, echoed in a wounded voice, "Seven Dials? I don't know what you mean. Didn't you hear what

I said? I'm Lady Victoria Arbuthnot, and I've been——"

"And I'm Bonnie Prince Charlie," the Runner said kindly. "Go on home with you, girl. And for heaven's sake, put some clothes on. You'll shame your poor mother, dashing about in next to nothing like that. Not to mention catch your death."

"But——"

The Runner paid no heed. He gave Victoria another push, this one not as gentle, then turned and started back down the street, whistling his happy tune. Victoria stared after him with a look of utter despair.

It was only when a couple happened by on the other side of the street—a well-dressed man and woman—that Victoria realized how she must look to people. The woman, catching a glimpse of her, said, "Tsk-tsk!" in a loud voice, and the man put his arm protectively around her, as if he feared Victoria might fly at them with a pick-ax.

Victoria was shocked. Surely no one could possibly think she'd *chosen* to dress this way. But apparently these hardened Londoners thought exactly that. Why, they must have thought her a madwoman, or—and here Victoria had to swallow hard—something even worse.

Her cheeks scarlet, Victoria darted back into an alleyway, this one some streets over from the one that had led from the back of Lord Malfrey's house. Good Lord, what was she going to do? She had no idea where she was, and not the slightest idea of how to get home. She was cold and wet and her feet were beginning to hurt, and everyone in London seemed to think she was a madwoman. What in heaven's name was she to do? She might, she could not help thinking, have leaped straight from the frying pan and into the fire. For while the idea of having to marry Lord Malfrey was repugnant, to say the least, being mistaken for a madwoman in the streets of London seemed infinitely worse!

And just when Victoria had begun to believe she had sunk to an all-time low, she heard a sound that caused her blood to curdle. And that was a man's voice, just behind her, that said, "Well, well, what have we here?"

Thinking it was Lord Malfrey, and that she was well and caught, Victoria closed her eyes and uttered a quick and silent prayer for strength. If she screamed, she wondered, would the Runner come sprinting back and save her? She doubted it. She had no choice. She was going to have to face the fact that she couldn't run anymore, and that there was no help to be had in the city of London for a woman wearing only her underthings and a blanket . . . even if that woman happened to be a duke's daughter.

Swallowing hard, Victoria turned to face her tormentor . . .

. . . and found herself staring not at Lord Malfrey, but at several children who appeared to be as dirty and raggedly dressed as she was.

"See here," demanded the eldest of the children, the

one whose voice she'd mistaken for Lord Malfrey's. And indeed, it did belong to a man, but one who was only teetering on the brink of adulthood. "What are you doing in these parts? This here is *our* turf, understand? You go on back to your own part of town, or we'll teach you quick."

Victoria, not having the slightest idea what the boy was talking about, put up a hand to sweep some of her uncombed hair from her face.

"Please," she said in a tired voice. "I would love to go back to my part of town. Only I don't know how to get there, and no hacks will stop for me."

The boy's eyes widened perceptibly. "Gor!" he cried. "Is that you, miss?"

Victoria blinked at the young man, who'd grown visibly excited, while his companions did not express nearly as much enthusiasm.

"I'm not sure," Victoria said. "Do I . . . do I know you?"

"It *is* you!" the boy cried. "You remember me, I know you do! From last week, in the park?"

Suddenly Victoria recognized him. It was the footpad, the one who'd attempted to steal Rebecca's reticule.

"You!" Victoria cried. "Good heavens! How do you do?" And she stuck out her right hand politely.

If the footpad was surprised by this nicety, he didn't show it. He pumped her hand eagerly in his own, and said to his friends, "This is her! That lady I was telling you about. The one what helped me go free when the other gents were about to send for the Runners."

The three other children murmured solemn greetings but continued to eye Victoria with suspicion. Victoria learned why when the second-eldest one said, "But, Peter, you told us she was a great lady wif a parasol."

Peter—which was apparently the footpad's name—nodded. "She were! I mean, you were, weren't you, miss? But . . . if you don't mind me saying . . . did you lose the parasol?"

"And the rest of your clothes?" chimed in one of the younger children.

"Oh," Victoria said, her heart welling over with gratitude that finally, finally someone was willing to listen to her. "Oh, yes. You see, it's been so dreadful. I was abducted by a very horrid man. Well, not abducted, exactly, since I went with him willingly enough. But only to give him his letters. And then we got caught in the rain, you see, and his mother said she'd put my clothes aside to dry, only then she wouldn't give them back to me, and they locked me in this little room, and I've only just escaped and . . ." Here Victoria paused to draw a ragged breath. "And I would be so very grateful to you if you could help me get home."

The youngest of the four children tugged on the shirt of one of the others and asked, "What's 'abducted'?"

"Never mind," Peter said grandly. "Of course we'll help you, miss. You helped me, so we'll help you." Looking down at Victoria's mud-encrusted feet, he observed, "But you won't get far on those. What do you say we nip 'round the corner to our place, and you can rest a bit, and maybe get those toes of yours cleaned up?"

"Oh," Victoria said, nearly weeping in gratitude. "That would be lovely."

Then, offering her his arm as if he were the dandiest of gentlemen, Peter, followed by his little entourage, escorted Victoria to his "place," which proved to be a very small and run-down room in the cellar of a very small and run-down building some blocks away. The room smelled a bit gamily of cat—indeed, there were several with whom the children seemed to share their domicile—but Victoria supposed the cats at least guaranteed the absence of rats.

The room was, however, warm and dry, and brightly lit by dozens of candle stubs . . . rather the way Victoria had always imagined Ali Baba's cave. She was offered a cup of hot—though very weak—tea, which she drank thirstily and gratefully as she looked about her.

"Do you all live here?" she asked, since there was a homey look about the shabby room. Ragged pieces of laundry hung from the ceiling, and there were several pallets lying about, which looked comfortable enough.

"Oh, yes," Peter said, clearly proud of his home. "Pay our rent just like anybody. It's right snug in winter, and very private."

Victoria, who'd been offered a bowl full of not very

clean water to soak her feet, bent to scrape some of the mud off them before dipping them into the basin. "And where are your parents?" Remembering what the footpad had told her at the time she'd caught him, her eyes widened. "They weren't *all* hanged, were they?"

"Naw," Peter said, much to her relief. "But Pa, he drinks. And Ma . . . well, we don't know where Ma disappeared to."

"Parents," said one of the younger children scoffingly. "Who needs 'em!"

Since Victoria, being orphaned herself, could well understand this sentiment, she did not reply, but said instead, "But surely there are safer ways to make a living than robbing people in the park. Couldn't you . . . I don't know . . . work as a chimney sweep or something? At least that way you wouldn't need to fear arrest."

Peter looked contemptuous. "Chimneysweep? You got to be an apprentice to get work like that. Ain't no one going to apprentice the likes of me."

Victoria put her feet into the water, and was surprised to find that they stung a bit. She must, she realized, have cut them on something.

"I don't see why not," she said, ignoring the pain. "You seem a bright enough boy."

"Oh, he's bright," one of Peter's siblings assured her. "But he's a thief."

That, apparently, was all the explanation Victoria was

to get on the matter. Peter, it was clear, had tired of the subject, and now presented her with a stub of pencil and a torn piece of foolscap, on the back of which was someone's grocery list. A sensible boy, Peter had evidently found and saved the scrap of paper for just such an occasion.

"I thought as you'd like to get a message to someone, miss," he said in a gentlemanly tone. "Tell me where to take it, and I'll deliver it."

One of Peter's siblings objected to this very generous offer, but Peter soon cut him off with a whispered, "Are you dense? She's bound to send it to some toff who'll give me a guinea for it."

This sounded to Victoria a very practical plan. She said, "Indeed, he'll likely give you a whole pound, as well as a ride back." Then, taking the pencil, she wrote carefully:

> *Something rather dreadful has happened. I am*
> *all right, but would you please come away at once with*
> *this young man and fetch me? And tell no one about it.*
> *Oh, and please bring with you a gown and a pair of*
> *shoes (any kind will do).*
>
> *Yours Truly,*
> *V. Arbuthnot*

There was not room on the foolscap for more, or she might have explained herself better. She folded the note and handed it to Peter, and mentioned an address. Peter nodded, seeming to know the place well, and assured her he would be back in a flash.

Then he left, leaving her in the less-than-tender care of his siblings, who seemed to find nothing at all odd about having a lady dressed only in a blanket and her undergarments in their bedroom. Indeed, they seemed to take the situation very much in stride, and only asked Victoria a searching question or two about whether or not she could read. When it was established that she could, they handed her a pamphlet and asked her to tell them what it said.

Which was how, when Jacob Carstairs arrived a half hour later, he found the Lady Victoria Arbuthnot reading aloud to three ragged street urchins from an abandoned racing form.

CHAPTER SIXTEEN

There were, of course, any number of other people to whom Victoria might have dispatched her plea for help. There was her uncle Walter, for instance. There was Mr. Abbott. There was Captain White, from the *Harmony*. There were any of the other numerous gentlemen with whom she'd become acquainted since arriving in London.

But Victoria had thought of one name and one name only when she'd determined that a gentleman must be sent for, and that name had been Jacob Carstairs.

And that was, purely and solely, because he was the only person Victoria knew who could be counted upon to keep his mouth shut about Lord Malfrey and what he and his mother had attempted to do to Victoria. After all, the captain had managed to keep secret for this long what the earl had done to his sister. It seemed likely he would not go bleating around London regarding Victoria's predicament, either.

It was vital, of course, that news of what Lord Malfrey had attempted to do to Victoria not get out. Mr. Gardiner, with all his harumphing, was bound to insist on going to the police. Captain White, being a military man, was likely to do the same. And as for Charles Abbott . . . well, Victoria would sooner have died than made him party to anything so sordid. His wedding to Rebecca was in only a few weeks. Nothing must happen that could delay—or, perish the thought, cancel—it.

No, the only person Victoria even thought of contacting was Captain Jacob Carstairs.

But even so, she was not *happy* about the arrangement. She was not looking forward to having Jacob Carstairs, of all people, rescue her from her current situation. She could only imagine the barbed comments such a discovery was bound to elicit from him. He would, she knew only too well, have a good deal to say on the subject of girls who went alone to exchange letters with their former fiancés, and probably something or other to say about girls who accepted horseback rides from said fiancés during thunderstorms, as well.

No matter. Victoria felt she could bear anything—anything at all—if it meant she could get home without further mishap . . . and that the Gardiners—and anyone else, either, for that matter—would never discover the truth about her adventure.

Still, though she had felt herself prepared for Jacob Carstairs's censure, she was certainly not expecting his complete and total shock at finding her sitting in her undergarments in a squalid thieves' den.

"Victoria!" he cried upon ducking beneath the tattered blanket that served as a doorway to Peter's lodgings and spying her on the opposite side of the room—a room he crossed in a mere three strides. "My God! What on earth. . . ?"

Victoria had been telling herself, ever since Peter had gone away to fetch him, that Jacob Carstairs seeing her in her underclothes was not the worst thing that had ever happened. They were, after all, still *clothes*. She was still *dressed*. She just had rather less on than usual. Still, her body was covered, for the most part.

So why he had to look so very scandalized, Victoria could not imagine. Why, he was even *blushing!* Jacob Carstairs! If it hadn't all been so absurdly embarrassing, she might have laughed.

As it was, however, she merely stood and, holding the blanket about her as tightly as she could, asked, "Did you bring me something to wear?"

"What?" the captain asked, still looking very red in the face, and apparently not knowing where to put his gaze. Then he seemed to remember himself, and thrust at Victoria a brightly colored bundle.

"Oh, yes," he said. "Here. I don't know what's there, exactly. I just went into my mother's closet and seized the first thing I could find."

"This will do nicely," Victoria said, seeing that he had brought her a day dress in sprigged violet, and a pair of rather dainty-looking dancing slippers. Then, noticing that he still stood staring at her, she snapped, "You needn't gawp like a beached salmon. Turn around."

Captain Carstairs, going redder than ever, obliged her, laying a firm hand on his young escort's shoulder and spinning him around as well. Victoria handed the corners of her blanket to two of Peter's siblings, whom she assumed were both girls, as their hair was on the longish side, and they obediently held the cloth as a sort of dressing screen while Victoria slipped on the violet gown and carefully laced up the slippers. Both gown and shoes were too large for her, but as everything that needed to be covered was so, Victoria felt satisfied. She did wish she had a comb and a looking glass, so that she might do something about her hair, but she hadn't mentioned either of those things in her note, and she doubted even Captain Carstairs, who seemed an eminently sensible young man, aside from his collar points, would have thought of them.

"Victoria," Jacob said to the wall he faced, "are you going to tell me how you got here, of all the places in the world, and where, in the name of God, your clothes are?"

"Well," Victoria said, rapidly doing up the buttons of Mrs. Carstairs's gown, "it's rather a long story—"

"She was abducted," one of Peter's sisters chimed in helpfully.

"Abducted!" Jacob was so startled he started to turn around, but a bark from Victoria stopped him. "Abducted?"

he said in a quieter voice, addressing the wall once more. "By whom? Victoria, what is that child talking about?"

Victoria sighed. She could see nothing else for it. She was going to have to tell him. Smoothing the violet gown, she said to Peter's sisters, "It's all right," and they lowered the blanket. Then, to Captain Carstairs, she said, "You can turn around now."

Jacob did so, but if she'd expected any compliments from him—such as, "That color looks lovely on you," or even, "That's better"—she was destined for disappointment, since he said only, "Dash it, Victoria, can we go now? This place . . . well, it's"—a glance at Peter caused him to modify whatever it was he'd been about to say—"a little depressing."

"Oh." Victoria looked at her small host and hostesses. "I suppose so. Did Captain Carstairs pay you for your efforts on my behalf, Peter?"

"Five whole pounds," Peter replied in a proud voice that indicated those five pounds were the most money he had ever had altogether in his entire life . . . and judging by the looks on the faces of his sisters, when they heard the vastness of the sum, it would not last long.

"It was all I had on me," Jacob said uncomfortably, misinterpreting the looks.

Victoria extended her hand to the head of the family, who took it in his and shook it energetically, and assured Victoria that if there was ever anything else she needed, she was to look him up. Victoria assured him that she would, and with a last concerned look about the room in which she'd been so graciously received, she allowed Captain Carstairs to escort her to the enclosed carriage he had waiting outside.

"Jacob," she said as he handed her up into the seat, "I feel terrible leaving those poor children there all by themselves. I feel as if we should *do* something for them. Don't you have any openings in your offices for anything? Messenger boys, or something? Couldn't you give Peter an apprenticeship or something?"

"Victoria," Jacob said in a manner that gave her the distinct impression that he was gritting his teeth, "I am not about to start taking footpads into my employ. Before we go about saving all the orphans of London, supposing you tell me just what, precisely, happened to you this evening? Where are your clothes? You do know that your aunt and uncle have been sick with worry, don't you? And what is all this talk about abduction?"

"Well, I'll tell you," Victoria said as Jacob sank down in the seat beside her, then rapped on the ceiling of the carriage to let the driver know he could move on. "But you've got to swear you won't start shouting at me. I've had a perfectly horrid night, and I won't stand being shouted at."

"I thought you said," Jacob Carstairs reminded her dryly, "that it isn't polite to swear."

Victoria flicked an irritated glance in his direction. It

was difficult to see him, given the darkness of the carriage, but she could make out his profile well enough in the moonlight spilling through the windows.

"Very well," she said. "You've got to *promise* me, then."

"I'll do nothing of the sort," Jacob Carstairs said. "If you've done something worthy of being shouted at, I have every intention of shouting at you until I am hoarse. I may shout at you even if you haven't done anything worthy of it. Have you any idea, Victoria, what a scare you gave everyone? Your aunt and uncle contacted my mother frantically at nine o'clock this evening, wondering if we'd heard from you. They seemed to think you'd been struck by lightning and killed during that thunderstorm this afternoon. . . ."

"Well, I wasn't," Victoria said. "But that isn't a bad idea. We can tell them that I was, and that my clothes caught on fire, and that some kind citizens found me and took me in and that I only just regained consciousness. . . ."

"Victoria." Now she was certain Jacob was gritting his teeth. "I am a patient man, but—"

Victoria could not help letting out a snort at that. "You? Patient? That's rich."

"Victoria. Just tell me what happened."

And so Victoria, keeping her shame-reddened cheeks turned resolutely away from him—though it was doubtful that he'd even have been able to see them in the darkness—told him everything. She told him about having gone to meet Lord Malfrey, and about the storm, and about being consequently conveyed by the earl to his rooms.

This last caused the captain to utter a curse that fairly burned her ears.

"Lady Malfrey was there!" Victoria hastened to assure him. "Only . . . well . . ."

And then Victoria had no choice but to relay the shameful truth about the dowager's part in her betrayal. When she came to the part about Lady Malfrey's refusal to give back her clothes, Jacob burst out with, "Victoria! How could you be so stupid?"

Victoria did not think this at all fair. How was she to know the dowager, who had been so kind to her in the past, had no heart to speak of, and was willing to stoop to such duplicitousness in order to see her son advantageously married?

"Because I told you so!" Jacob burst out when she voiced the thought.

"You told me only that Hugo Rothschild was a rogue," Victoria pointed out to him. "You told me he hadn't any honor. You didn't mention that he was a foul kidnapper and a blackguard."

"Next time," Jacob said, sounding very much affronted, "I'll make myself more clear. Well, go on. Tell me the rest of it. But I'm warning you, Victoria, if he laid a finger on you . . ."

Victoria felt a curious thrill upon hearing Jacob threaten bodily harm to the earl, but told herself it was only because Lord Malfrey so justly deserved a thrashing. She was forced to assure him, however, that the earl hadn't so much as touched her—she left out the part about him lifting her bodily and throwing her across the bed—because she didn't want Jacob to fly into a passion. Though personally it would not have troubled her a bit if he did so—it actually would have been quite entertaining—she did not want her aunt and uncle to see it, since she wanted to keep from them the awful truth about what had happened to her. And they were, as she spoke, getting closer and closer to the Gardiners' town house.

"And then I simply climbed out the window," Victoria finished, drawing her story to a rapid close, as she had begun to recognize the street upon which they'd turned as the one belonging to her aunt and uncle. "And ran about trying to get someone to help me, which was no joke, let me tell you. Londoners seem a very suspicious lot, I must say. The only people who believed I really was Lady Victoria Arbuthnot and not a madwoman escaped from an asylum somewhere were Peter and his sisters, and they only believed me because Peter recognized me. . . ."

Victoria's voice trailed off as the carriage pulled to a halt in front of her aunt and uncle's home, and she realized that Jacob Carstairs was staring at her with a somewhat indescribable look upon his face. She could not tell whether he was horrified or admiring. In case it was the former, she reached up quickly and began to pat down her hair.

"What is it?" she asked. "Do I really look such a fright? Why didn't you tell me before? I don't want to scare them, particularly if the little ones are still up. You wouldn't happen to have a pocket comb about you, would you? Or would your driver, perhaps? Though I suppose if I *were* struck by lightning, my hair would be sticking up a bit, wouldn't it?"

Jacob Carstairs, however, surprised the life out of her—not by handing her a comb, which really would have been incredible—but by doing something even more shocking. Instead he laid a hand on either of her shoulders and pulled her rather roughly toward him, then kissed her squarely on the mouth.

Victoria had time to think, *Oh, no, not again,* before giving herself over to the kiss. Because, much as he annoyed her, being kissed by Jacob Carstairs really was one of the most wonderful things in the world, quite equal to, in Victoria's opinion, champagne and even ices.

She wasn't at all certain why Jacob Carstairs was kissing her—certainly it wasn't because she was looking so very irresistible. Victoria was fairly certain she had dirty smudges on her face—until he thrust her roughly away from him and said, giving her a shake, "Climbed out the window! Victoria, you might have been killed!"

"Well, yes," she said, a little disappointed that the kissing had stopped. "But it was quite easy, because I didn't look down, the way you said—"

And then, happily, the kissing continued, and Victoria could not help thinking that really, for so aggravating a person, Jacob Carstairs could be quite comforting when he chose to. It was a pity, in fact, that he didn't choose to be so more often. She was feeling supremely comforted by the time Jacob lifted his head and said, "Damn," beneath his breath, adding, "I suppose we'd better go in."   .

Victoria was so comforted by that point that she supposed she'd have followed Jacob Carstairs into the mouth of a volcano if he'd asked her to. But he only pulled her out of his carriage and up the steps to her aunt and uncle's house.

There, despite the lateness of the hour, everyone in the household was up, waiting frantically for news of her, from her uncle Walter to Cook to the ferret. There were a great many cries of, "Where have you been, Vicky?" and "We were worried sick!" from Mrs. Gardiner, and a good deal of harumphing from Mr. Gardiner. The younger children leaped about with joy, while Rebecca joined Cook in weeping tears of happy relief, and Clara looked dejected upon learning that nothing worse had happened to her cousin than a dunking in the river. For it had been decided by Victoria and Jacob on the doorstep that her story was to be that she'd taken a fall into the Thames, losing her reticule and ruining her clothes and shoes, and that a kindly but non-English-speaking fishing family had scooped her out, and not been able to understand Victoria's pleas that a message be taken to her family.

It was not a very good story—Victoria felt that the lightning one was far better—but it was the only one Jacob would agree to stick to. And so she told it with great gusto, embroidering on it for Clara's benefit by saying that the fisherman had had a dark and surly son who'd tried to make her eat a bowl of macaroni. Clara was very impressed by this, as she was suspicious of foreigners and quite despised macaroni.

"But however did Captain Carstairs find you?" Mrs. Gardiner wanted to know, and Jacob replied that he'd ridden out to look for Lady Victoria, and happened upon her near Hayter Street. The gown and shoes she wore, Victoria informed them, had been donated by a vicarage near there. She'd been trying to find a hack when Captain Carstairs had miraculously appeared in the moonlight.

It was the most ridiculous story ever told in the history of time. If Victoria had tried to feed it, or anything like it, to her ayah, she would have received an icy stare and a "Try again. The truth, this time."

But the Gardiners, who were for the most part an easygoing lot, took it in stride, and, satisfied that a happy ending had been achieved, began to drift sleepily off to bed. Victoria herself would gladly have followed them, had she not noticed a determined look in Jacob Carstairs's eyes as he took his hat and gloves back from Perkins. She had no choice but to linger in the foyer and hiss, as Jacob started for the door, "Where do you think you're going now? And you had better say home."

Jacob shot a wary look at Victoria's uncle, who was harumphing his way up the stairs to his bedroom. "Then I suppose I had better not say at all."

Furious, Victoria reached out and pinched the captain's arm, hard enough for him to jerk it away with an irritated expression. "Victoria! What is wrong with you? That hurt!"

"You had better not be going to Lord Malfrey's," Victoria whispered angrily.

"What if I am?"

"Jacob!" Victoria glared at him. "Don't you dare. Not a breath of this must get out, do you understand? And if you go over to Lord Malfrey's and start a fight, or challenge him to a duel, or anything stupid like that—"

"Stupid!" Jacob interjected. "I'll tell you what's stupid. Stupid is—"

"Vicky?" Rebecca called sleepily from the stairs. "Are you coming to bed?"

"Yes, Vicky," Mrs. Gardiner said with a yawn. "Come along. You can finish thanking the captain tomorrow."

"Stupid," Victoria said in a hiss to Jacob, ignoring her relatives, "is you doing anything that might cause even a hint of what happened tonight to get out."

"Victoria," Jacob said in tones of great weariness, "you said it yourself. The man is a blackguard. He's got to be stopped. And if I'd done it the first time, when he broke things off with my sister, none of this—which is ten times worse than anything he did to Margaret— would have happened."

"And if you do it now," Victoria whispered urgently, "Becky's life will be ruined."

"*Becky?*" Jacob Carstairs looked down at her as if she were mad. "What are you talking about?"

"Her wedding," Victoria reminded him. "To Mr. Abbott! Jacob, you can't challenge Lord Malfrey to a duel. If it were to get out, people would know it was over me, and what happened to me tonight will become public knowledge, and I'll be ruined, and then Mr. Abbott might call off the wedding."

"Blast Charles Abbott!" Jacob said, with feeling. "If he calls off the wedding, that's his own idiocy. I can't do anything about that. And how could you be ruined? You were an innocent victim!"

"Vicky!" Mrs. Gardiner called from the second floor. "Say good-night to Captain Carstairs and *come to bed.*"

"Promise me," Victoria said, reaching out and laying a hand upon one of his. "Please, Jacob. Promise me you won't do anything rash."

Jacob looked down at her fingers resting so lightly over his, and said, with enough heat that Perkins, busy dousing the flames in the chandelier above their heads, glanced over, "You seem a good deal concerned about Mr. Abbott. What about me?"

Victoria blinked up at him. "What *about* you?" she asked, really not having the faintest notion what he was talking about.

"If I challenge Malfrey, I might be killed, you know," Jacob informed her with some bitterness. "You might show *some* concern for my life."

Victoria, highly amused by this, said with a laugh, "I might, indeed, if I cared about you."

At which point, much to her surprise, Jacob settled his hat upon his head, dropped her hand, and said in a cold voice, "Well, I'm certainly glad we've got *that* straight," and stormed out the door.

Victoria watched him go with raised eyebrows and a bemused expression. What a strange and abrupt young man he was! She supposed that, judging by what Rebecca had told her, he'd have preferred to have found her swooning and teary-eyed over what Lord Malfrey had done to her. And she supposed if she'd clung to him and begged him not to go after the earl, it might have been more effective than asking him not to kill him for Mr. Abbott's sake.

She probably *could* have shown a little more gratitude for his coming out in the middle of the night to fetch her. . . .

But hang it, none of it would have happened in the first place if he hadn't insisted on her breaking her engagement with the earl!

Really, Victoria thought wearily as she turned around and headed at last for the stairs and for bed. Men were excessively tiresome creatures. Particularly the ones with whom one couldn't help but fall in love.

She was nearly to the landing before she realized what she'd done, and when she did, she gasped as if she'd been stung by a wasp, and flung a hand to her throat, causing Perkins to ask worriedly if she was feeling well.

"Oh," Victoria replied. "Perfectly well, thank you."

Except, of course, that she was lying. She wasn't perfectly well at all. Not when she'd realized the horrible, glaring truth at last.

She was in love with Jacob Carstairs!

CHAPTER SEVENTEEN

Well, it wasn't as if he hadn't warned her.

One day, Lady Victoria, he'd told her, *you're going to meet a man whose will can't be bent to suit your purposes. And when that happens, you'll fall in love with him.*

How infuriating—how perfectly nauseating!—that he had been right. She *had* met a man whose will she couldn't bend, no matter how hard she tried—and Lord! How she'd tried. And she had gone and fallen in love with him.

How she could not have realized it until it was, in all likelihood, too late, Victoria could not imagine. Everyone had been telling her she was in love with Jacob Carstairs—or, at least, Rebecca had—but she'd refused even to entertain the thought. Her, Lady Victoria Arbuthnot, in love with a man who called her names, and did not in the least know how to dress? Perish the thought!

But there it was, obvious as the nose on her face. Why else did his kisses make her feel so . . . well, comforted? And why else had he been the first person she'd thought to contact when it had come time to write a note back in Peter's little hovel?

But most of all—and this was the thought that

rankled hardest, that kept her up, even tired as she was, half the night, when she should have been dead to the world after her ordeal—why else had she agreed to marry the ninth Earl of Malfrey in the first place?

Oh, her cheeks burned even in the darkness of her own bed as she thought of it. But it wasn't any good pretending it wasn't true. She had already admitted to herself that she had said yes to Lord Malfrey's proposal to vex the captain. She'd wanted to make him jealous. Why?

Because, irritating and impossible as he was, she was in love with him . . . had been in love with him, probably, since the first moment she laid eyes on him.

But how was such a thing even possible? Why would she fall in love with such a man? Jacob Carstairs didn't need her. His life was perfectly in order, his affairs laid out neat as the pins in Victoria's workbox.

And he was always very rude to her, teasing her, and making light of her very serious calling, which was, of course, to manage the affairs of others.

But he had been right about one thing, Victoria realized blearily in the wee hours of the morning. And that was that her own affairs were in a perfectly disgraceful state. Particularly if she went about falling in love with men who didn't need her.

But wanted her. He had said that the other day, the day he'd asked her to marry him. That he didn't need her, but that he wanted her just the same. He seemed to think wanting was better than needing, but Victoria hadn't been so sure.

Now, lying in her bed, listening to the steady breathing of Rebecca in the bed beside hers, Victoria began to wonder if perhaps she hadn't been too hasty when she'd turned down Jacob's proposal. Oh, it hadn't been a proper proposal . . . there'd been no moonlight or flowers, let alone a ring. She hadn't felt she'd had any choice, of course, but to say no.

But now . . . How very different she felt! If Jacob were to propose to her on the morrow—even a flippant proposal—even if he called her Miss Bee and made buzzing noises, as he did sometimes—Lord help her, but she might . . . she *would* . . . say yes.

Only he wasn't going to propose to her on the morrow. Why should he? He had already warned her once that he wasn't going to ask her to marry him again. Badly as she'd treated him—and except for the kisses, she had treated him very badly indeed—she didn't exactly blame him. What kind of man went about constantly proposing to a girl who kept turning those proposals down? Worse, who accepted the proposal of his worst enemy?

Oh, no. Jacob Carstairs would not propose again.

And that was why Victoria lay awake half the night, wondering how on earth she was going to get herself out of *this* particular mess. Because Jacob had been quite right when he'd said there was one person whose life was a perfect shambles, and who dreadfully needed the management skills of Miss Bee: and that person was herself.

Only it was so different when it came to one's *own* affairs! Victoria was perfectly comfortable telling other people—her uncles; her aunt; her aunt's cook; her aunt's children; the hostesses at Almack's; everyone, really—what to do. But when it came to herself—at least insofar as concerned Jacob Carstairs—she seemed completely incapable of making the correct decisions. If she had simply been honest with herself from the beginning, none of this would even be happening. She, like Rebecca, would happily be planning her wedding . . . and this time, to the *right* man.

But instead she found herself tossing and turning half the night away, wondering how on earth she was ever going to get Jacob Carstairs to propose to her again.

Morning found Victoria, instead of well rested and calm, irritable and short-tempered. She snapped at poor Mariah—who really was making remarkable progress, for a maid who'd started out as such an incompetent—half a dozen times as she was arranging Victoria's hair. And then she shouted at Jeremiah, who'd thoughtlessly left a toy wagon on the stairs that Victoria had nearly tripped over. Was this, she could not help wondering, what love—true love—did to people, then? Turn them into nasty-tempered shrews?

She supposed so. Unrequited love, anyway. Because

that was what hers was, until she could see Jacob again and explain herself. For though Victoria would never have advised anyone else—Rebecca or Clara or any girl, for that matter—to be truthful with the object of her affection in regards to her feelings, all the rules went right out the window when it came to herself. She was going to tell Jacob Carstairs everything the first moment she saw him. So what if he held the information like a whip over her head for the rest of her life? Victoria, so used to telling others what to do, was beginning to think she might enjoy being bossed about a bit for a change.

But as the morning wore on, and there was not a single call or note from Captain Carstairs, Victoria began to worry. Surely he ought to have written, if not stopped by in person. Where on earth was he?

The more Victoria wondered, the more she remembered the unpleasant way they'd parted the night before. Jacob had been most put-out with her for her lack of concern over his personal safety. *You might show* some *concern for my life,* he'd complained.

And what had she done to soothe his wounded feelings? Why, poured salt into them, of course!

I might, indeed, if I cared about you. That's what she'd said! What a wit! What a fool! Now he might never come calling again, and he would be perfectly justified. Why, he might very well choose simply to ignore Victoria altogether from now on! He might never call her Miss Bee or laugh at her—or kiss her—again! How would she bear it? How on earth would she bear it?

When they had received no word from him by eleven o'clock the morning after her escapade in the back alleyways of London, Victoria—though no one else in the household, of course—began to grow truly alarmed. This simply wasn't like Jacob. He seemed always to be hanging about, saying disparaging things about her needlepoint and hauling the younger Gardiners about on his back. Where was he? Was he really that angry with her?

Flummoxed, Victoria did the only thing she could think of: she bundled up the gown and slippers Jacob had lent her the night before, and sent them, along with a note, to the Carstairses' residence. The note, over which she agonized for an hour, said:

> *Dear Jacob,*
>
> *Enclosed you'll find the things you so generously loaned me last night. I cannot thank you enough for your kindness in coming to my aid in my hour of need. You were a true knight-errant, and I will be forever in your debt. Please forgive any impertinence on my part, as I was overtired after my ordeal.*
>
> *Yours very truly,*
> *V. Arbuthnot*

Victoria had hesitated over the address. Should she call him Captain Carstairs? Weren't they, by now, on a first-name basis with each other? The man had, after all, seen her in her undergarments.

And the part where she'd apologized for her flippant remark about not caring for him . . . was that not specific enough? Perhaps she ought to have mentioned the *exact* impertinence for which she was asking forgiveness.

She hoped that the *Yours* very *truly* would make it clear to him that she had had a significant change of feeling toward him . . . or rather, not a change of feeling, because she felt she'd always loved him. She just hadn't admitted as much to herself until now.

Then she told herself she was being ridiculous. It was only a *note*, after all, not the Magna Carta. She needed to calm down. She needed simply to send the package and wait for his reply.

She sent the package.

When, by four o'clock, no response had come—no note; no letter; and certainly not Jacob Carstairs himself—Victoria began to wonder if something hadn't happened to him. Supposing, on the way home from the Gardiners' house the night before, his carriage had met with an accident and turned over, and Jacob was even now lying crushed beneath the wheel spokes!

But no, she supposed if there'd been an accident like that, she'd have heard. Jeremiah and his brothers were very keen on carriage accidents, and scoured the neighborhood daily in search of them.

Then, at five o'clock, an even worse thought occurred to Victoria: supposing Jacob had, in spite of her warnings, gone ahead and challenged the earl! Supposing he was lying dead in Hyde Park even now, with a bullet to the heart!

Oh, no! Surely not! Surely if Jacob and Lord Malfrey had dueled, she'd have heard about it by now. Mrs. Carstairs would have written to tell them the unhappy news. . . .

Besides, if Jacob and the earl were to duel, Jacob would surely win! Why, Lord Malfrey was a coward who tried to trap innocent heiresses into marrying him! Surely a man like that would never win a duel, not against a man who had single-handedly built up his father's shipping business into a company worth forty thousand pounds, if not more. . . .

"Heavens, Vicky," Rebecca said as the two of them were changing into their ball gowns—for it was Wednesday, and Wednesday meant Almack's, rain or shine, dead lovers or not. "You're skittish as a cat." For Victoria, hearing a bell ring downstairs, had rushed to the window to see if Captain Carstairs's carriage was below. But it was only the iceman. "Are you certain you're all right? You didn't catch a cold from your fall in the river, did you?"

Victoria, woefully eyeing her reflection, thought to herself that if Jacob Carstairs really had been killed by Lord Malfrey, she would have to purchase all new gowns.

For even though she wasn't married to him, she would *feel* like a widow.

"I'm all right," Victoria murmured in response to her cousin's question.

"Well, you don't look it," Rebecca generously assured her. "Pinch your cheeks a bit. There, that's better."

"Becky." Victoria stared at her cousin's reflection in the mirror. "Remember when you said that you thought Jacob Carstairs was in love with me?"

"Mmm-hmmm," Rebecca said, donning one of Victoria's sapphire ear bobs, and admiring the way the gems glittered.

"And that you thought perhaps I was in love with him?"

"Yes." Rebecca pinched her own cheeks. "What about it?"

"Oh," Victoria said, then sighed. "Nothing."

Rebecca turned to look at her, her fair eyebrows raised.

"Victoria!" she cried, her eyes glittering as brightly as the sapphires in her ears. "You *do* love him, don't you?"

"No, I don't," Victoria said quickly. "I don't, really." Then, realizing what she was saying, she buried her face in her hands. "Oh, all right. I do. I do, and it's too late, because I've been so horrid to him! Oh, Becky!"

And suddenly all of the tears that had been absent during Victoria's breakup with Lord Malfrey came spilling out in torrents reminiscent of the Ganges during monsoon season.

"Vicky!" Rebecca had never seen her younger cousin in tears, and did not know what to do about it. "Oh, Vicky! My dear! Don't cry! Oh, he loves you, I'm quite certain of it. He rescued you from those dreadful fishermen last night, didn't he?"

This only served to make Victoria weep even harder. Rebecca, at a loss, ran for her mother, who came away from her dressing table only half-dressed, and did what mothers are supposed to do when they see one of their children in pain: she folded Victoria to her copious bosom and said, "There, there, now. It will be all right. All the excitement has finally caught up to her, I think. You'll stay home tonight with a hot brick, I think."

Victoria, horrified, quickly extricated herself from her aunt's arms and said, "No, no. I'm all right. I've got to go to Almack's. I've *got* to!"

Because if she were ever to see Jacob Carstairs again, it would be at only one place, the place where everyone gathered every Wednesday night. And that place was Almack's.

"I don't think you'd better, child," Mrs. Gardiner said worriedly. "You look worn out. Wouldn't you rather stay here with Clara and the younger children and—"

"No!" Victoria nearly choked. "No, no!"

Mrs. Gardiner regarded her curiously, then shrugged and said, "Suit yourself. But hurry up, girls; we leave in half an hour."

Half an hour was not enough time for Victoria to calm

her spirits and repair the damage her tears had done to her face. And it was not enough time for Rebecca to come to terms with this new creature—a cousin Vicky who cried, and over, of all people, Jacob Carstairs, who'd once been her sworn enemy. It was therefore a solemn group that arrived that night at Almack's . . . though Rebecca's equanimity was soon restored by Charles Abbott, who stepped forward to claim her at once for a quadrille. Victoria was left to prowl the rooms, searching for one face—one single face—and not finding it.

"He isn't here," she wailed to Rebecca when the latter stepped off the dance floor to retie her shoe. "Captain Carstairs isn't here!"

"Well, of course not," Becky said. "It's early yet, Vicky. Don't worry."

But her cousin didn't understand. She hadn't heard what Victoria had said to Jacob the night before. And she didn't know about Lord Malfrey, and the possibility that Jacob might be lying dead from a bullet to the brain *at that very moment!*

And the fact that Lord Malfrey himself had yet to show up was no comfort to Victoria. What kind of man would dare show his face at Almack's after the horrible thing he had tried to do to her? No, it was no wonder Lord Malfrey was nowhere to be seen. But Jacob was another story. Victoria had never known him to miss a night. He could only be staying away because he was dead . . . or because he hated her. Either way Victoria was wretched, and she turned down each and every man who approached her to ask for a dance, until finally Mrs. Gardiner sidled up to her and said, "My dear, I know you are still heartsore over your broken engagement with the earl. But don't you think you ought to give one of these other nice gentlemen a chance? For you are very young, my dear, and will learn to love again. . . ."

It was somewhat ironic that at the moment these words were coming from Mrs. Gardiner's lips, in through the doors came striding a man with collar points that were far too low to be stylish. Victoria did not have to see the face of the owner of those collar points to know to whom they belonged. Only one man in London wore his collar points so unfashionably low.

And it was toward this man with a glad cry that Victoria rushed.

CHAPTER EIGHTEEN

"Captain Carstairs," Victoria said, hurrying to Jacob's side. "Good evening."

He looked down at her. If there was a touch of surprise in those sardonic gray eyes, he did not express it. He acted as if Victoria came rushing across dance floors to greet him every day of the week.

"Lady Victoria," he said with icy politeness.

That politeness, as no unkind word could have, cut Victoria like a knife. Polite! Jacob Carstairs? To *her*? Oh, the situation was very bad indeed! Worse even than she'd allowed herself to imagine. A bullet was really the only thing that could have been more terrible.

Fear clutching her heart, Victoria did the only thing, really, that she could have, under the circumstances. And that was grab Jacob by the arm and drag him into the closest alcove, where they could have it out at last.

"Victoria," Jacob said, sounding considerably annoyed as she shoved him behind a velvet portiere, where they were shielded from the prying gazes of Almack's other patrons. "Good Lord, what is the matter?"

Victoria could not believe he could just stand there

and ask what was the matter when all day long she'd felt as if her heart were breaking.

"What is the *matter*?" she demanded. "*What is the matter?* Why didn't you answer my note?"

He shrugged, trying to put his coat to rights after the way Victoria had pulled on it in order to get him into the alcove. "Why should I have?" he asked. "I knew I'd see you tonight."

Victoria narrowed her eyes at him. "Oh, you knew you'd see me tonight, did you?"

"Why do you keep repeating everything I say?" Jacob wanted to know. "And why do you look like that?"

Victoria's hands went instantly to her face. "Like what? What are you talking about?"

"I don't know," Jacob said. "You look . . . flushed. It isn't any wonder after everything you went through last night. You're probably feverish. Your aunt and uncle oughtn't to have let you come. I'd better have a word with them—"

"Jacob!" Victoria cried, furiously stamping her foot.

He gave her a curious look. "What is it now?"

"Why are you acting like this?" she demanded.

"Like what?" He looked genuinely blank.

"So . . . so polite?" Victoria pointed her fan at him threateningly. "You'd better stop it. I told you I was sorry in my note for what I said last night."

One corner of his mouth went up. But the other one

stayed down. "So you did," he said. "Although you neglected to mention just which of the many unpleasant things you said to me last night you meant."

"You know perfectly well which one I meant," Victoria said haughtily. "Don't make me say it."

"Oh, I think you'd better," he said, folding his arms across his chest. "I think you owe me that much, at least."

Knowing that she was blushing furiously, but unable to do anything about it, Victoria said, with her gaze on the floor, "I'm . . . I'm sorry I said I didn't care about you."

But Jacob wasn't satisfied. He continued to regard her with his arms folded. "Because . . . ?"

"Because . . . I do. Care, I mean. A little."

"A little."

"Yes." She looked up and felt a wave of righteous indignation sweep over her as she saw that he was smirking. "Well, I hope you don't expect me to say that I love you, after the way you've treated me!"

"The way *I've* treated you! Oh, that's rich. And how have I treated you, except far better than you deserved?"

Victoria snorted. "Please! Calling me Miss Bee, and telling me what to do, and then . . . then leaving me alone all day long without a word! Jacob, I thought you might be dead!"

"Dead?" He seemed, if she wasn't mistaken, to be enjoying himself no end. "Why on earth would you think that?"

"Well, because you didn't come see me, and you didn't answer my note, and . . . well, you know. Lord Malfrey."

"Ah, yes." He did not look so pleased anymore. "Lord Malfrey. Well, Victoria, it might interest you to know that the reason I did not stop by or answer your note is because I was busy. Busy dealing with friends of yours, actually."

"Friends of mine?" Victoria looked astonished. "But who on earth . . . ?"

"Young Master Peter, for one," Jacob said. "I've offered him an apprenticeship in one of my offices, and my offer was, you'll be happy to hear, accepted."

Victoria wasn't certain she had heard him correctly. "You . . . you *what?*"

"Well, I gave it some thought and decided you were right. We couldn't leave those children in that cellar. One of my clerks has taken him and his sisters in. They have plenty of room; their own son is commanding a ship of mine headed for the West Indies. Peter and his sisters seemed to be settling in nicely when I left them. Mr. Pettigrew and his wife are terribly fond of children. But I'm afraid I had to draw the line at taking in the cats. . . ."

Victoria gazed up at Jacob in utter astonishment. She really was not at all certain that she believed what her ears were telling her. "But . . . but . . . I thought . . . I thought you'd gone to shoot Lord Malfrey."

"Oh, I thought about it," Jacob admitted. "But it didn't seem worth it. Despite the fact that you didn't seem to put much value on it, I like my life, and was loath to risk giving it up for a blighter like Malfrey."

"Oh, Jacob," Victoria began, tears filling her eyes exactly as they'd done in Rebecca's bedroom earlier that evening. "I never—"

"No, I had a better idea," Jacob said. "I went to Lord Malfrey and made him—and his mother—an offer they couldn't refuse."

"An offer?" Victoria stared up at him, puzzled. "What kind of offer?"

"Well," Jacob said amiably, "I told them I'd give them free crossing to France on one of my ships, if they promised never again to set foot in London."

Victoria blinked, forgetting about the tears beneath her eyelids. One drop slid out, and fell, unheeded, down her cheek.

"Why," she heard herself asking, "should they accept such an offer? Oh, Jacob, I hope you didn't tell them that if they didn't, you'd go to the magistrates. I don't want anyone to know what happened to me! And if it should get out—"

"No, no, have no fear for your precious Mr. Abbott. I said nothing like that." Jacob reached into his waistcoat pocket and drew out a handkerchief, which he handed to her as matter-of-factly as if he were handing her a cup of tea. "I told you I had a very busy day. Before paying my call on the Rothschilds, you see, I paid a visit first to the consistory courts."

"The consistory courts?" Victoria shook her head. "But what—"

"Oh, they keep records there," Jacob informed her conversationally. "In Doctors' Commons. Quite remarkable, really. Anyone can stroll in and look at them. Takes some doing, and it's quite dusty work, but do you know my persistence paid off? I came across the most curious fact about your Lord Malfrey."

"He isn't *my* Lord Malfrey," Victoria snapped.

"He most certainly isn't. He belongs—or should I say belonged—to one Mary Gilbreath."

Victoria forgot her annoyance over his having called Lord Malfrey *her* Lord Malfrey and asked curiously, "Who is that?"

"Don't you know? I'm rather surprised you don't. But then, India is a large country, and you might not have happened to run into her. Mary Gilbreath is—or rather was—the first Lady Malfrey."

Victoria knitted her brows. "You mean . . . the dowager was the eighth earl's second wife?"

"Not at all," Jacob said. "Mary Gilbreath was Hugo Rothschild's first wife."

"Wife?" Victoria was so shocked she had to grab hold of the velvet portieres to keep from falling over, as there

was no chair nearby to sit upon. "Hugo has been married before?"

"Oh, yes," Jacob said, clearly enjoying himself. "Shipboard wedding, don't you know. Not on one of my ships, of course, or I should have been aware of it. No, but he did do it on his way out to India, after throwing over my sister. Miss Mary Gilbreath was an heiress, rather like . . . well, you . . . who was on her way to visit relatives in Bombay. She became the first Lady Malfrey en route."

Victoria said, "But then . . . then Lord Malfrey is a widower? How did she die?" She sucked in her breath. "Oh, Lord, Jacob! He didn't kill her, did he?"

"Good heavens, no," Jacob said. "You really do have a morbid imagination, Victoria; has anyone ever told you that? Malfrey's a rogue, but he isn't a murderer. . . ."

"Well," Victoria said, feeling a bit nettled by his teasing. Then again, what else was new? "What happened to her, then?"

"Nothing happened to her, least as far as I know," Jacob said. "I suppose Malfrey ran through all her money—he would. He had his mother to support, too, don't forget, back in England. And then he left her."

"His mother?"

"No, Victoria. Mary Gilbreath."

"Left her? Left his wife?" Victoria, startled, cried, "Then he's a bigamist?"

"Nothing quite that dramatic, I'm afraid," Jacob said

with a grin. "They're divorced."

"Divorced?" Victoria felt as if she'd been struck. "Lord Malfrey . . . *divorced?*"

"Yes," Jacob said, appearing to take pity on her. "They keep divorce records at the consistory courts, Victoria. That's why I went there. I had a sneaking suspicion about your Lord Malfrey. And I'll admit . . . I'd heard rumors."

"That he'd divorced his first wife?"

"Rather the other way around, I'd wager," Jacob said. "But that's the way the records read, anyway. Lord Malfrey divorced his wife, undoubtedly collecting a tidy sum from her relations, who surely paid for the proceedings, as divorce is expensive, as you know. But the poor girl's family probably would have paid anything to be rid of the blighter. I know I would have, if it had been my sister."

"But . . ." Victoria murmured. Divorces, she knew, were not awarded lightly in the British courts, and were expensive and rare for that reason. "But . . . why on earth did he come back to England? He had to have known someone would find him out. . . ."

"I suppose he ran out of money," Jacob said. "He must have gotten a bundle from the Gilbreaths, but he squandered it. I know he was in Lisbon to buy a horse—"

"A horse!" Victoria shouted. "He told me he went there to buy back some family portraits!"

"Well, he didn't," Jacob said dryly. "You've got to admire the man, in a way. He was running low on funds, and was surely worried that once he was back in England his secret might get out. The girl's family must have paid handsomely to keep news of the divorce from leaking into the papers. It helped, of course, that they lived abroad. Still, anyone might learn of it, if they bothered to look the way I did. The earl had to marry quickly—for once they were wed, of course, there'd be nothing his bride could do, short of divorcing him herself—before someone found out about Mary. It was quite a stroke of luck for him, running into you on the *Harmony*."

"Oh, yes," Victoria said bitterly. "Lucky for *him*." She kept her gaze on the toes of her slippers. She could still not quite believe what she'd heard. Divorced! The Earl of Malfrey! The man she'd come so close to marrying!

And that Jacob Carstairs, of all people, should have been the one to have found it out. It was too much. Really, it was all too much for her.

"Well, to make a long story short," Jacob went on, "I paid a call to the earl a little while ago and informed him that unless he wanted his secret to be made public knowledge—which would, as you know, ruin him for this season's crop of heiresses, as there isn't a sane mama in the world who would allow her young daughter to marry a man who'd been divorced in such a manner—he and his mother had better decamp for the continent. They were both only too willing to oblige. I suppose they'll make haste for the Riviera. There are probably quite a few wealthy widows there who wouldn't mind marrying a younger man—even one with such a past."

Victoria, still staring at her feet, felt a tear slide from the corner of her eye, slip down her nose, then drop to the floor. *Perfect.* She was crying again. Why? There wasn't anything to cry about. Lord Malfrey was gone, and good riddance to him. So why on earth . . .

"Here, here," Jacob said, reaching out suddenly and lifting her chin, so that she had no choice but to meet his gaze. "What's this? What are you crying for? Don't tell me—Victoria, you can't still be in love with that conniving ass, can you?"

She sniffled woefully. "No," she said.

He took the handkerchief from her fingers and dabbed her cheeks with it. "Well, what is it, then, Miss Bee?"

Miss Bee! He had called her Miss Bee! Perhaps all was not lost. . . .

"It's just . . ." Victoria said, with another sniff. "The only reason I agreed to marry him in the first place was because I . . . I . . . was so angry with you for . . . well, you know. Calling me M-Miss Bee instead of—"

"Flattering you and murmuring tender words of love in your ear, the way Malfrey did?" Jacob finished for her. "But Victoria, I knew perfectly well you'd never fall for that sort of thing. Not for long. Look how long you and Malfrey lasted. And I wanted you for keeps."

Victoria sniffed some more, despite the fact that her

heart was suddenly soaring. "But . . . " she said. "But you were so nasty!"

"So were you," he reminded her.

"Only because you would never do as I said. And you know, aside from this thing with Lord Malfrey, I *am* right, Jacob, most of the time, about most things. You must admit, the food at the Gardiners' table *has* improved since I took over planning the menus. And Becky *is* engaged. And my uncle *is* more talkative. If more people would simply do as I tell them, their lives would be a thousand times nicer."

"Yes," Jacob said solemnly. "I'm certain that's true. And you're welcome, Victoria, to manage as many people's lives as you like. But not mine, thank you very much."

Victoria bit her lip. "Are you certain? Because, you know, I think with very little effort you could be immeasurably improved. Your collar points, for instance." Her heart slammed so hard against her ribs that it hurt, but she really felt she *had* to say it. "Why do you wear them so low? Everyone else wears theirs a good two inches higher. If you would just—"

"Yes," Jacob said. "But when anyone else goes to kiss the woman he intends to marry, his collar points stab her in the face. Is that what you want?"

Victoria, remembering suddenly that kissing Lord Malfrey had been a little uncomfortable because of that very thing, began to think that Jacob might be right. She was even more convinced when he followed up this illuminating statement with a physical demonstration of his point.

No, most decidedly, Victoria was delighted to learn when Jacob kissed her, his collar points did not get in the way in the least.

Then, even as Jacob was making a more thorough investigation into the veracity of his theory, Victoria tore her lips from his and said in a shocked voice, "Jacob! You said . . . you said when a man kisses a woman he intends to marry. Does that mean that . . . do you intend to marry *me*?"

"I most certainly do," Jacob said in a firm voice. "What do you have to say about that, Miss Bee?"

But Miss Bee didn't answer, because she was entirely too busy kissing him.

2

DEAR READER:

You've got to love how Vicky just can't stop thinking about Captain Carstairs. She may have thought it was his abominably low collar points (clearly a crime against 1810 London fashion), but it was obviously something else entirely.

All of the Avon True Romances tell the story of a girl, a guy, and how they get together, often against seemingly insurmountable odds. While a few of the heroines are wild, others possess a quiet grace. And while some of the heroes are wickedly charming, some are noble and true.

Turn the page for a complete list of the books. Read them and find out what kind of love story *you* like the best!

Abby McAden
Editor, Avon True Romance

AVON TRUE ROMANCE

SAMANTHA AND THE COWBOY
by Lorraine Heath

Samantha meets her cowboy on the plains of 1860s Texas on a wild, western cattle drive that will have hearts racing.

BELLE AND THE BEAU
by Beverly Jenkins

Belle escapes from 1850s slavery in Kentucky and makes it to Michigan, only to catch the eye of a beau—only he's someone else's beau. But not for long . . .

ANNA AND THE DUKE
by Kathryn Smith

Anna is engaged to be married—a dream come true for a girl of 1818 Regency England—but when a handsome stranger strides into her life, Anna's life is turned upside down, and not unpleasantly.

GWYNETH AND THE THIEF
by Margaret Moore

When Gwyneth stumbles upon an unconscious thief near her castle in 1202 England, she doesn't see him as a threat, but she does not anticipate what occurs between them, either.

AVON TRUE ROMANCE

NICOLA AND THE VISCOUNT
by Meg Cabot

In Regency London, every girl wants to make a good match. Nicola thinks she's done it with the fabulously handsome (if conversationally challenged) Viscount Sebastian Bartholomew. Turns out she's wrong . . .

CATHERINE AND THE PIRATE
by Karen Hawkins

It is 1777, and Catherine is desperate to get to Savannah from her native Boston—so much so that she hires a pirate to take her. But is this young man interested in more than her money?

MIRANDA AND THE WARRIOR
by Elaine Barbieri

It's 1852, and before defiant seventeen-year-old Miranda knows what has happened, she's nabbed by a celebrated Cheyenne warrior who is just as stubborn as Miranda.

TESS AND THE HIGHLANDER
by May McGoldrick

In 1543, on a windswept isle off of Scotland, seventeen-year-old Tess finds a young man half alive in a tidal pool while a great storm rages around them. Little does she know he holds the key to her mysterious past . . . and her heart.

AVON TRUE ROMANCE

EMILY AND THE SCOT
by Kathryn Smith

Emily is a proper English miss who dreams of marrying a dashing, wildly romantic Scot. Fleeing scandal in London, she travels to the Highlands in 1819. She finds her true love, but he isn't exactly how she imagined him. . . .

AMELIA AND THE OUTLAW
by Lorraine Heath

Amelia is the apple of her father's eye, and doted upon by her two big brothers. But when an outlaw named Jesse strides into their lives in 1881 Texas, nobody can keep her from him.

JOSEPHINE AND THE SOLDIER
by Beverly Jenkins

Josephine is a young woman with a sassy look and a sharp tongue, especially, it seems, where Adam is concerned. He may be a Union soldier in the War Between the States, but that doesn't mean he's Jojo's hero. Or does it?

VICTORIA AND THE ROGUE
by Meg Cabot

Victoria has managed to arrange herself a marriage to a most suitable young earl. But is he suitable? And why can't she stop thinking about the entirely unsuitable Captain Carstairs? (To find out, turn to page 1 and start reading, of course!)

And truly, if you enjoyed *Victoria and the Rogue* and *Nicola and the Viscount*, it would be a shame to miss any of the other books by #1 *New York Times* best-selling author Meg Cabot:

THE PRINCESS DIARIES

THE PRINCESS DIARIES, VOLUME II:
PRINCESS IN THE SPOTLIGHT

THE PRINCESS DIARIES, VOLUME III:
PRINCESS IN THE LOVE

THE PRINCESS DIARIES, VOLUME IV:
PRINCESS IN WAITING

PRINCESS LESSONS:
A PRINCESS DIARIES BOOK

ALL-AMERICAN GIRL

HAUNTED:
A TALE OF THE MEDIATOR